Mud Happens

Mud Happens

Bill Swan

James Lorimer & Company Ltd., Publishers
Toronto

James Lorimer & Company Ltd. acknowledges the support of the Ontario Arts Council. We acknowledge the support of the Government of Canada through the Book Publishing Industry Development Program (BPIDP) for our publishing activities. We acknowledge the support of the Canada Council for the Arts for our publishing program. We acknowledge the support of the Government of Ontario through the Ontario Media Development Corporation's Ontario Book Initiative.

Cover illustration: Steven Murray

The Canada Council | Le Conseil des Arts
for the Arts | du Canada

ONTARIO ARTS COUNCIL
CONSEIL DES ARTS DE L'ONTARIO

Library and Archives Canada Cataloguing in Publication
Swan, Bill, 1939-
  Mud happens / Bill Swan.
(Sports stories ; 82)
Sequel to: Mud run.
ISBN-13: 978-1-55028-899-5 (bound)
ISBN-10: 1-55028-899-7 (bound)
ISBN-13: 978-1-55028-898-8 (pbk.)
ISBN-10: 1-55028-898-9 (pbk.)
  I. Title. II. Series: Sports stories (Toronto, Ont.) ; 82
PS8587.W338M833 2005   jC813'.54   C2005-904865-4

James Lorimer & Company Ltd.,   Distributed in the United States by:
Publishers   Orca Book Publishers
317 Adelaide Street West   P.O. Box 468
Suite 1002   Custer, WA USA
Toronto, Ontario M5V 1P9   98240-0468
www.lorimer.ca
Printed and bound in Canada.

Contents

For Kathy, with love.
Now it begins.

1

Home at the Dome

Outside the tent-like skin of the Oshawa Civic Dome, a January snowstorm howled. The air was cold enough to freeze snot on a shop teacher's moustache. Inside, Matt Thompson and members of his school running club were finishing a workout on the four-lane indoor track, sweating as though it was a fine day in June.

"Two more sets," Ms. Wellesley said. "Get ready in fifteen seconds."

Ms. Wellesley was Matt's eighth grade teacher and his track coach. Well, not the school's *official* track coach. But since the end of the cross country races in the fall, Ms. Wellesley had invited the interested runners from the S.T. Loveys Elementary School to join her at the Oshawa Civic Dome.

Overhead, the roof of the Dome shuddered in the wind. A clump of snow flapped loose from the roof fabric and began a slow, noisy slide to the ground. That's when Matt knew his secret desire was to join the Durham Riders Track Club.

The knowledge came, not as a niggling hint, but as a whole idea, full and complete. It landed on him in the same way four hundred pounds of snow had just slid from the roof and landed with a thud in the snowbank outside the air-supported Dome.

Matt did realize that his decision to join the Riders had something to do with the way Ashley Grovier watched Riders running. With lean, tight muscles, the high school runners bounded around the track like gazelles.

Ashley was a classmate in his eighth grade class, and also a member of the 100-Kilometre Club, the school's informal running club. She wore a different coloured hair band each day, and would often touch Matt's arm just before telling him something important — like "Hi!" or "Can I borrow your homework?" Matt had always liked Ashley's smile, and he also liked to have his arm touched.

Both he and Ashley had been members of the school's championship cross-country team that fall. It was because of that win the previous October that both were now at the Oshawa Civic Dome waiting for Ms. Wellesley to say "Go!" When she did, the club members would all run twice around the track at a pace fast enough to make the last-half lap difficult. *Really* difficult.

"Two more laps?" asked Ryan Abolins, his voice with an edge like a nail file even when he was being nice. Ryan had orange hair and nose rings. "Sure you haven't lost count?"

"Two more," repeated Ms. Wellesley with a big smile. "Your turn to lead, Ryan," she said. "If you're up to it. Baz will lead the last one."

Before they could step on the track, a group of five high school runners — all members of the Riders — surged by, running strongly.

"Wow! Look at them run," said Ryan. "I could run like that." He ran a hand through his orange, spiked hair. "Call me the copper-top bunny."

"Yeah, right, Rye," said Ashley. "As if."

"Ready, guys," Ms. Wellesley continued. To Ryan she said, "Now!"

Ryan started out, the others following behind like baby ducks behind their mother.

Matt pulled in behind Ryan. Baz Amin, his dark eyes sparkling, settled in just off Ryan's right shoulder. Though he couldn't see them, Matt knew Kathryn Lau, Ashley, Robert Maxwell, and Gavin Richards had taken their places behind him. As usual, Ms. Wellesley would be at the back of the pack, calling directions if needed.

Not that much direction was needed anymore. Ms. Wellesley organized routines that kept all the runners together as a group, yet challenged even the best runners before each workout ended.

Behind him, Matt could hear Ashley complaining.

"My Gawd!" she gasped, though she was never as breathless as she pretended to be. "I mean, wait up!"

Matt smiled, knowing that the others behind them were beginning to string out as the pace took its toll. Even Baz, who always looked so relaxed, had tightened his shoulders. On the curves, Matt could see the corners of his mouth pulled back in concentration.

"It's not a race, Ryan," Ms. Wellesley called from the back of the group. "Even pace, even pace."

As they came up the final straightaway for their first lap, the group from the Riders pulled up on their right, then began to easily pass them.

Matt could sense the Riders before he could see them: five, no, six of them — five guys and one girl — all two or three years older. These were elite athletes. They were fitter and faster than him, faster than Ms. Wellesley had them running.

Matt knew that Ashley was watching them, too.

Matt worked hard. Baz, just off his right shoulder, breathed in grunts. But Matt felt good. He put all his focus into maintaining his pace. Ryan was also running strongly, two metres ahead.

The high school runners eased by, their strides smooth, graceful, and effortless.

Matt checked over his shoulder. From the corner of his eye he could see Ashley and Gavin Richards, and behind them, Ms. Wellesley. Along the straightaway, he could see the Riders' coach, clipboard held in the crook of his left arm.

At that moment, Matt made a decision. In an instant, he moved ahead of Baz. Within three strides he'd pulled even with Ryan, who flashed one look at him before responding with his own surge.

But Matt had the momentum and eased ahead, his quickened pace and longer strides bringing him even with the last-in-line of the Rider runners. Between gasps, Ryan uttered a word that should never be said in public.

Off the curve under the four-handed clock, Matt pulled up behind the last of the high school group. He struggled now to keep up. Ryan followed, grunting, but was unable to catch him.

Matt gritted his jaw, his long legs reaching, his arms pumping hard. He couldn't gain on the high school runners. But they weren't pulling away from him, either.

Halfway up the final straight, Matt knew he was dying.

His legs turned into tree trunks. His lungs began to burn. His arms became heavy, leaden limbs, like tree branches with no bark. For a moment he lost sight of Ryan.

But two steps later Ryan suddenly reappeared in the corner of his eye. He struggled hard, grunting like an elephant.

Matt wasn't going to let Ryan beat him.

He dug even deeper, every muscle now screaming, his fists balled up, white with effort. This was his time to show off. To Ashley. To the coach. To the Riders. No one would beat him now. Especially Ryan.

One step, two step, three step, four…

They finished their two-lap interval in one-two order, twenty or more paces ahead of Baz, with the rest of the group strung out further back, Ms. Wellesley half a lap back.

"Did you … see … that!" Matt exclaimed, drinking in air by the lungful. "I kept … up with … those … guys!"

"I was right with you!" said Ryan, bent over, hands on his knees, sucking air.

Almost a half-minute later, Ms. Wellesley floated across the line with Ashley, Kathryn, and Robert.

"Even pace, Matt," she said. "The idea is to do an even pace. Not race."

"But I … can run … that … fast."

"For a lap," said Ms. Wellesley. "Which isn't the same thing. Look — those high school runners are still going. They've got two more laps to go."

"Actually, just four and a half," said a man with a clipboard at the side of the track. "They're doing one kilometre repeats today." Ms. Wellesley looked at the man.

"Thanks, Joe," she said. "These guys just sometimes get carried away."

Joe waved his clipboard as though to say, "So what, don't worry." Matt knew from being around the track for several months now that this was Joe Calder. He was the coach of the Riders, a high school teacher, and a former running star himself. At least, that's what everybody said.

"We'll take a couple of minutes before we do our last interval, then we'll warm down," Ms. Wellesley said. She came over to Matt. "That's not a good team move," she said. "When we do group intervals like this, keep the pace even."

"I just wanted to see if I could run that fast," Matt replied, still gasping.

"Well, you can," said his teacher. "But with middle and long distance it's how long you can run at that speed. Endurance. That's what these intervals build."

"It felt good." Matt panted. "Nobody could keep up with me." He glanced over to see if Ashley had noticed, or had overheard him. He breathed deeply. Ryan was still bent over.

"We're about to start the last interval," said Ms. Wellesley. "Be ready. Right after the Riders come by again."

Joe Calder moved forward. With a sweeping motion of his clipboard, he eased Matt and Ryan back off the track. "Watch out," he said. "They're coming around again in these outside lanes. We don't want anybody hurt."

Ms. Wellesley herded her group under a soccer net that had been parked on the outside of the track.

"Still think you could run with those guys, Matt?" asked Baz.

"Maybe someday you will," said Ms. Wellesley. "But they are among the best high school runners in the country. Last year, two of Joe's runners made it to the World Cross-Country Championships."

"Did you say ... the World?" asked Ryan, still breathing deeply.

Matt saw Ashley watching the group of five runners at the far side of the track.

"Yes, the World. Quite a few national level athletes have worked out on this track.

"Did you run with the Riders, Ms. Wellesley?" asked Gavin. "You were a champion."

Ms. Wellesley smiled, her eyes still on the track. "I'm a runner, always," she said. "Winning a race or being a champion lasts only for a day. Running is for a lifetime. Now let's watch the traffic here before we begin our last interval."

The practices in which two or more track clubs worked out always created traffic problems. Casual runners, including tennis players, who often jogged two or three warm-up laps, used the two inside lanes. Sometimes they would wave their rackets around while they ran, adding a layer of excitement. Track clubs used the outer two lanes for doing speed intervals. And sometimes the sprinters cluttered up the track with starting blocks, or step-kick training along the straightaway.

The high school runners came by again.

"On pace," Joe Calder said, one eye on his stopwatch. "Keep it up."

The Riders galloped by like frisky ponies. Matt envied them. He pictured himself in high school, training with runners like them, winning races and perhaps someday running for Canada. Maybe Ashley would, too, and they could go to the movies after the races.

Joe Calder turned to Ms. Wellesley.

"When are you going back to train with the Riders?" he asked.

The previous fall, Ms. Wellesley had injured her leg running a race in Toronto. When Matt had started at S.T. Lovey, she had been limping.

"Soon," she said to the coach. "I thought I had given that ankle enough rest back in the fall. But then I did that cross-country thing at Hyde Park.

"I remember that," said Joe. "Won that, didn't you? I thought you were ready then."

Ms. Wellesley grimaced. "It's the old story: too much, too soon. I'm going to try something in the all-comers meet a week Saturday. We'll see how it goes then."

"No rush," said Joe. "When you're ready."

Matt had been listening to this conversation while watching the Riders still on the track.

"They're … still … at it," Matt said, between deep breaths.

"You going to be okay?" Ms. Wellesley asked him. "Are you enjoying the sensation of oxygen debt?"

"What's oxygen debt?" asked Gavin.

"What Matt and Ryan are going through. Breathing hard. Going faster than you can sustain."

"Oh," said Gavin, as though he understood.

"Okay. Ready?" Ms. Wellesley continued. Matt nodded. "Baz, you lead this time."

Baz grinned. He made a good leader. He could maintain an even pace through both laps. His black hair gleamed.

"And Matt," she added, "stay behind the leader."

Matt laughed.

"Now!"

Baz leaned forward and was off running.

Matt pulled up just off his shoulder, with Ryan behind. That was the advantage of the intervals, he thought. As in a race, leading a group was hard work. Even running steady, sixty second laps, following someone else was always easier.

Baz took them through the first of the two laps at exactly sixty seconds. Halfway through that first lap, Matt had begun to work. He focused on the back of Baz's shoulder. As they started the second lap, Baz began to pull ahead. Ryan pulled up even with Matt's shoulder.

Baz continued to pull away from both of them. With half a lap to go, Matt ran stride for stride with Ryan. His legs felt heavy, his breathing laboured. Beside him, Ryan made grunting noises.

From the back of the pack, Ms. Wellesley called out, "Good pace, Baz, good pace. Come on, Matt, Ryan. You're fading!"

Matt worked harder now than ever. Still, Baz continued to pull away. He and Ryan continued, lagging behind. Breath came hard. Every step took effort. From thirty metres back, Matt watched Baz cross the finish line. Finally, Gavin Richards, the kid from the fourth grade, pulled up even with Matt at the finish line.

Ms. Wellesley and Ashley followed close behind.

"Still want to know what oxygen debt is, Gavy?" Ms Wellesley asked. "Ask Matt and Ryan. They'll tell you."

"I beat 'em, I beat 'em!" said Gavin.

"Only because they both tried to keep up with the Riders on the previous interval," said Ms. Wellesley. "Now everybody come on over here. I've got some news about an all-comers meet a week from Saturday."

2

Family Thaw

"The upstairs toilet won't flush."
Cathy-Marie, Matt's older — and only — sister, made the comment to Matt and their mother as soon as they stepped into the front hall.

"Tell your father," said Mrs. Thompson. "I don't do toilets."

"I did but he …"

"Take care, take care, take care," said Mr. Thompson, emerging from the lower level of the house. He carried his tool box and a long-cord power bar wound around one shoulder.

"Your hair dryer up there?" he asked, indicating both his wife and daughter, and pointing to the bathroom.

"Now's not the time to dry your hair, father dear," said Cathy-Marie, sarcastically. "Or did you get the message? The toilet won't flush." Cathy-Marie was completing her last year of high school. Increasingly, Matt had noticed, she and her father argued about everything.

"Interesting, isn't it?" Mr. Thompson said. "Today's females. They're all about equality and stuff. But as soon as a toilet won't work, who they gonna call?"

"Father! That is the most, most, most…" Cathy-Marie's face twisted in anger.

"The most prejudiced, that's the word you're looking for," said Mr. Thompson. "Now, have you any idea why the toilet won't flush?"

"I … I …" Cathy-Marie fell silent.

"The water line is frozen again!" said Mrs. Thompson. "That's the third time this winter. Questions we should have asked when we bought this house."

The Thompsons had moved to Courtice in August, when Mr. Thompson had started a new job as a graphic designer.

"Really, Mother! Your husband is such a, such a, such a …"

"Forty years ago, the term you are looking for would have been 'male chauvinist,'" said Mrs. Thompson. "But I don't think that fits here, anyway. Don't confuse task preference with gender equality.

"If you like, I can make dinner while you look after that … job," she said to her husband.

Mr. Thompson shrugged. "I got home early and put a meat loaf in the oven. You can scrub some potatoes while I look after this." He indicated the tool box and power bar.

"Want me to help?" asked Matt. "Last time I held the hair dryer."

"Great offer. Thanks. But this time I think Cathy-Marie has offered."

"You're kidding, right? Mom, he's kidding, isn't he? I don't know a thing about plugged toilets."

"Stuff happens," said Mrs. Thompson from the kitchen.

"Anyway, the toilet is not plugged," repeated Mr. Thompson. "The water line's frozen. And if you're going to be an independent woman someday, you've got a lot to learn. If Matt can peel potatoes and do dishes, you can learn about plumbing. You picked out your universities yet?"

Cathy-Marie would graduate from high school in June. For

the past few weeks, she had been worrying her parents about her university applications.

"I've already applied for three," she replied. "If you had paid attention last fall when I told you, you would know that."

"But have you picked out a favourite?"

"It doesn't work that way, father dear. At this stage I have to be accepted by the university."

"So who would want you?" joked Matt.

"Knock it off, you two," said Mr. Thompson. "Come on, give me a hand. Both of you."

The bathroom was small, but not cramped. Mr. Thompson put his tool box on the floor. "You know why this toilet won't work?"

Cathy-Marie shrugged.

"You said the water line's frozen," Matt replied. "Just like last time. So we just heat it up with the hair dryer. Right?"

"Every time it gets cold like this," Mr. Thompson said, "and we get a wind from the northwest, this happens." He plugged in the hair dryer and turned it on.

"Somewhere down in there…" he said, pointing at the wall and the levels below, "a section of the pipe is frozen. The only way to fix this is to blow hot air on it." He eased out the flange around the pipe feeding the toilet tank, and nestled the mouth of the hair dryer against the small opening where the pipe fed into the drywall.

He handed the dryer to Cathy-Marie.

"That's it?" she said, turning on the hair dryer. "We just blow hot air here…" she pointed to where the pipe disappeared into the wall. "And we hope that it gets to down there where the pipe is frozen?"

"There's your lesson about life. Things happen. You deal with the bad stuff when it comes up, and try to plan so it doesn't."

"Why don't we just call a plumber? I mean, duh."

"Sure, at a hundred dollars a pop. Think hundred-dollar bills come out of taps?"

"Not when they're frozen!" replied Matt.

"Yeah, yeah," said Cathy-Marie. "Now you're going to give me the guilt trip about what it will cost to send me to university."

"I wasn't going to mention that," said Mr. Thompson. "Just take this as a lesson in life."

"What do you mean?" asked Cathy-Marie.

"Stuff happens. Water pipes freeze. Life is not perfect. Sometimes you can fix things up with a hair dryer. Other times you have to rip off all the drywall and insulation to get at the heart of the problem."

Cathy-Marie flashed angry eyes at her father. But she turned on the hair dryer and aimed it at the hole where the water pipe disappeared.

"There's a bright side," said Matt.

"What's that?" asked his sister, the dryer still whining in her hand. "I can't think of any right now."

"If the pipes burst," Matt said, "we'll know exactly where the cold spot is."

"There is that," replied his father. "Though I'd rather not find out that way."

3

Training Untracked

What does she want?" asked Baz Amin as they stood at their lockers during noon recess at school the next day.

"I don't know," replied Matt. "You heard the same announcement I did."

"Maybe we're going to get our track outfits," said Kathryn Lau, adjusting her ponytail.

"Which outfits?" asked Ashley, her ears perking up.

"The school outfits," said Kathryn. "Remember? The parent council was going to raise funds for sports sweaters for the whole school."

"Yeah, cool," said Ryan. "But we don't need them until track season."

"The basketball team would get them first. So that can't be what she wants to see us about."

"If you're talking about Ms. Wellesley," said Ashley, fidgeting with some books in her locker, next to Matt's, "she doesn't sound too happy about whatever it is."

"Well, duh," said Baz.

Ashley brushed a speck from her trendy new jeans. "Gawd! I look like Godzilla!" She preened in front of the tiny mirror on the inside door of her locker.

"Whatever it is, she could have told us in class," said Matt. "Or last night at the track." The group had been training at the Civic Dome Tuesday and Thursday afternoons since before Christmas break.

"Or waited until tomorrow," said Baz. "My dad says he'll drive tomorrow night." They all lived in Courtice. The Civic Dome was on the far side of Oshawa, a fifteen-minute drive — or a forty-minute bus trip. Usually, their parents took turns driving.

"Tell your dad to chill," said Ashley. "Ms. Wellesley wants to meet us in the classroom. Something's up, I'm sure."

"Maybe it's about the all-comers meet," said Baz.

"Sounds like fun. Could you imagine us doing something like that if Ms. Wellesley hadn't come to teach here?" said Kathryn. "We'd still be plugging along in the 40-Kilometre Club."

"It's the 100-kilometre club, dummy," said Matt.

"Don't bug me, Mr. Cool," replied Kathryn. "It was the 40-Kilometre Club first. Then Ms. Wellesley came and everybody ran the 40 kilometres. So it became the 100-Kilometre Club. Anybody seen Ryan? He wasn't at school all morning."

On cue, Ryan came around the corner from the main lobby. He limped noticeably.

"Whazzup?" said Baz. indicating Ryan's left leg. "You got a flat?"

"Tendinitis," replied Ryan.

"Big word," said Matt. "What's it mean?"

"Doctor says it's swelling where the muscle meets the bone. Maybe in the cartilage. Right near where I cut my leg. My dad says we should sue the school."

"Over you kicking in that glass door last fall?" asked Kathryn. "You're kidding, right?"

"Yeah, kind of," Ryan replied. But the tone in his voice said there might be more to his father's threat.

The group turned to look at the glass doors leading to the lobby. The previous fall, the day of the cross-country championship, Ryan had smashed the doors with a kick. He had lashed out in anger because Matt had been allowed to run with the cross-country team.

"Sure he's kidding," said Baz.

"The intervals did it," said Ryan, ignoring him. "Doc said I tried too much, too soon. Now I gotta take it easy."

"You can't run?" asked Ashley. "Rye, that totally sucks."

"Only for a week or so. Then I can start again. Slowly. Gotta stretch and do funky stuff like that."

"I know what you mean," said Baz. "My grandfather does that Tai Chi stuff, too." He kept a straight face for a moment before guffawing.

"Oh, sure, really funny," said Ryan, but he was laughing, too.

At that point Ms. Wellesley came down the hall. She carried a pile of assignments in one hand and her briefcase in the other.

"Good. Everybody here but Robert," she said.

"And Gavy," said Ryan.

"Right. Okay. Everybody into the classroom."

"Whazzup?" asked Ryan.

"You'll see," said Ms. Wellesley, without her usual smile. Ryan leaned against the wall, his left leg out behind him, knee forward, stretching.

"It won't move," said Baz. "Push all you want, but that wall is not going to budge."

"If I get it up to starting speed it will," said Ryan. "Otherwise, we'll have to call for roadside assistance."

"He's stretching his calf, goof," said Ashley, before she realized they both were teasing.

Gavy came bouncing into the room. He moved up, down, sideways, like a rubber ball, angling off in all directions.

"Gavin, Kathryn, Robert, Ryan, Matt, and Baz." Ms. Wellesley read off the names.

"Wutz it all about?" asked Ryan, the last to follow into the classroom.

Ms. Wellesley dropped her briefcase and unmarked assignments on the desk. She turned and half sat on the desk in an un-teacher-like pose.

"You'll see," she said.

The principal, Mrs. MacMillan, entered the room and quietly closed the door. They could all hear the latch click into place. Mrs. MacMillan was a tall woman with heavy glasses and plain black sensible shoes.

"Hey! I bet we get our uniforms!" said Ryan. "It's about the uniforms, right?'

Mrs. MacMillan smiled patiently. "The uniforms are in production right now," she said. "But we won't see them for another couple of months. You'll just have to be patient."

"They'll be ready for track, though. Right?" said Ryan.

"They should be," replied the principal. Matt could tell she was trying to steer the conversation from uniforms to something else. Matt suddenly had a feeling he did not want to know what the something else was. Mrs. MacMillan nodded at Ms. Wellesley, who began as though she had rehearsed.

"I need to talk to you all about our track club," she said.

"It's going to be great," said Baz. "That all-comers meet. We'll get to see how our training…"

Matt could see from the look on Ms. Wellesley's face, and the glance between the teacher and the principal, that the issue was more serious.

Ms. Wellesley spoke quietly. "It's about our Tuesday/Thursday club. I don't really know how to put this any other way…"

She paused.

"I can't coach you any more."

The playground chatter outside faded into the distance in the silence that followed.

"Can't coach us?" said Ashley.

"Why not?" asked Kathryn. "We're just starting to get good."

Mrs. MacMillan stood with her arms crossed.

"It's not something that any of us like," she said. "But the school board has ordered the track program to stop."

"Not run track?" said Ryan, his orange hair bristling. "That's stupid!"

"It's not the track," said Ms. Wellesley. "It's the running off school property."

"It's a liability issue," said Mrs. MacMillan.

"Well, our parents take turns driving," said Baz.

Mrs. MacMillan stood still, her mouth drawn into a tight straight line.

"It's a big insurance thing," she repeated. "I'm sorry. I know how much this meant to all of you. Even you, Ryan," she added, with a weak smile. "Running and track have provided the leadership this school needed. Ms. Wellesley and I are as sorry as you are that this has to end."

"No more training at the Dome?" asked Matt.

"No more training at the Dome," said Ms. Wellesley. "The school board has given orders."

"But that's …" Matt spluttered. He really didn't know what it was. The words wouldn't come.

Kathryn, who had been mostly silent, looked up from where she had been examining the toe of her left shoe.

"Does this mean the 100-Kilometre Club as well?" she asked.

"No, that shouldn't …" Mrs. MacMillan started to answer but from her eyes you could see she had doubts about that, too.

"But we run that off school property," said Kathryn. "Out on the sidewalks. Around the neighbourhood. Are they going to stop us doing that, once the weather turns nice?" The runners had used the Dome for their regular workout two nights a week during the winter months, when running on sidewalks could be dangerous.

"We may have to reconfigure that," said Mrs. MacMillan. "But that could be done on school property. Then it would be all right."

"Run two kilometres," said Ryan. "On school property. Back and forth between the portables. Yeah, right."

"But we'll have uniforms!" said Gavin, who hadn't said a word yet.

"Uniforms? Who cares?" Ryan snarled. "By the time track season comes around, we won't be able to run."

Mrs. MacMillan held up two arms in warning.

"Let's just make sure we all know what's at stake here," she said.

"Yeah, our running club is at stake," mumbled Ryan.

"What's at stake," continued the principal, "is this school. It's my job to run it. I know you have all enjoyed working with Ms. Wellesley. You've enjoyed the running club, the Kilometre Club… "

"The 100-Kilometre Club," said Kathryn. "It's the 100-Kilometre Club now."

"Yes. Well. That's been a great inspiration. You ran in that club and as result you finished well at cross-country. As result, Ms. Wellesley has generously offered to continue that through the winter. By taking you to the Dome."

"She doesn't take us," said Gavy. "We get rides."

"But you do go to the Oshawa Civic Dome. You may have noticed it's off school property."

"Duh!" said Ryan. Mrs. MacMillan wilted him with a glance.

"There can be no official school activities off school property without proper sanction," she continued. "And the board has ruled that your sessions at the Oshawa Dome are not school events."

"But …" someone said.

"There are no 'buts.' There's nothing I can do. There is nothing Ms. Wellesley can do. It's out of our hands."

"But we could go to the Dome on our own?" asked Ryan.

"Theoretically," said Ms. Wellesley. "But the Dome officials reserve the time slots on Tuesday and Thursday for track clubs only. You couldn't get in on your own."

"We couldn't?" asked Ashley.

"But we could run around the gym here at school — that would be no problem?" asked Matt.

"If Ms. Wellesley were willing, that would be fine," said the principal.

"Yeah. Running in the gym. Not exactly an indoor track, is it?" said Ryan.

"And you mean, come spring we may have to stay on school property for our runs?"

Mrs. MacMillan nodded. "That would be the safest way," she said. "Besides, the running teams exist only for the cross-country race and the annual track meet. It's not as though…"

"That sucks!" said Matt. "You think running is just a thing we go out and do twice a year! We train more than most hockey teams. We are a team. We are the Lovey Larks! Even if you and the board don't think so!"

Mrs. MacMillan locked eyes with Matt.

"I know you're upset," she said. "But mind your manners. And your language."

Matt met Ms. Wellesley's gaze.

"What about the all-comers meet?" he asked. "A week from Saturday? Does this mean we can't run in that?"

Ms. Wellesley smiled. "Nobody said that," she replied. "The S.T. Lovey track team, or the 100-Kilometre Club, or the Lovey Larks, or whatever we call it, cannot run off school property. But this is an all-comers meet. So I see no reason why you can't run. I can't supervise you, but with your parents' permission there should be no problem. Would you agree, Mrs. MacMillan?"

The principal smiled ever so slightly.

"It's the school team that can't run," she said. "But what you do on your own time on the weekend is up to you."

The group shuffled out in disappointment. Finally, Ryan headed for the door.

"First my leg," he shouted. "And now this!"

The old anger was back in his voice. He ripped open the classroom door and flung it back so hard it bounced off the door stop, the door knob leaving a small dent in the drywall behind the door.

This time, Matt knew how he felt.

4

All-Comers Meet

A s Matt Thompson trudged through the revolving door into the Civic Dome, Ashley pulled him by the arm and posed the question:

"Have you entered yet?"

"Just got here," Matt replied.

"Hurry up!" said Ashley, bouncing on the balls of her feet. A green hair band firmly kept the hair out of her eyes. At the back, her shoulder-length ponytail danced with her movements.

The Dome buzzed with activity. Several tube-legged tables had been set up on the tennis courts. Runners were lined up at each. Matt moved through the crowd. He held his track bag with a cramped wrist over his left shoulder. He twisted this way , then that, through the crowd.

Each of the tables had been labelled for a different event: 100 metre, 200 metre, 400 metre, 800 metre, 1500 metre, 3000 metre.

"What did you enter?" Matt asked, turning to Ashley. But she was gone.

"Going to try the 1500 metre?" asked Ms. Wellesley, who suddenly appeared at his side. She pointed to a lineup two tables over. "If you're ambitious you might try the 800, too. More than that would be stretching your conditioning."

The crowd made Matt feel excited, nervous — and fit enough to run every race. He let the comment go. He had been running with Ms. Wellesley and the others for three months — ever since the cross-country championship at Ganaraska Forest in October. Before that, they had run as part of the school's 100-Kilometre Club for five, maybe six, weeks. Yeah, he was in shape, all right.

"Maybe I'll try the 400 metre, too," Matt said. On the 223-metre track, the 400 wasn't even two full laps.

Ms. Wellesley stood a few feet away. She bent over to tie her shoelaces. "Your first meet, you don't want to try too much. Even in the slow heats, the 400 can get pretty fast," she said. "The joggers and fitness runners always go for longer stuff — like the 1500 metre and the 3000. That's the longest we go indoors. There will be enough runners that you won't get left behind. In the 400 ... ." She left the sentence unfinished.

Matt joined the line to register in the 1500. Around him, runners gabbed, jabbed, stretched. Baz nudged Matt with an elbow.

"There's Mr. Tuchuk," he said.

Matt turned. Tony Tuchuk, the custodian at S.T. Lovey Public School, stood beside the track. He wore an old-fashioned nylon track suit.

They caught his eye and exchanged waves.

"Don't tell me he's running," said Baz.

"Old Tuchuk? You got to be kidding."

Ashley flashed a smile at Matt. "But that track suit he's wearing!" she said. "It's so, so, retro. I just love it!"

Matt lined up to fill out his entry form for his race. He hesitated over which heat to enter. What had Ms. Wellesley told him? The slowest heat? But what was that?

"Not sure?" asked the woman at the table.

Matt nodded.

"The 1500 is six and three-quarter laps on this track," said the woman.

"We've been running one-minute laps," said Matt. "With a rest," he added.

"One-minute laps. With a rest." The woman appeared to be pondering.

"You might try the first heat," she said. "Six minutes or more. If you run faster, well, next time you'll move up a notch."

Matt looked at the list in front of the woman. Even reading upside down, he could see some of the other names on the list. Ashley Grovier. Kathryn Lau. He couldn't see Ryan's name, or Baz's.

A dim plan formed in his mind. If Ms. Wellesley couldn't coach them, he would need to impress Joe Calder enough to win an invitation to run for the Riders. That's what he had to do. He put his five-dollar bill on the table and leaned forward.

"Faster," he said, finally, his mouth dry and the words fuzzy.

"A faster heat?"

Matt nodded.

"Okay," the woman said, as though unsure. "Next heat up is five to six minutes. Pretty broad range.

"Faster," Matt repeated, though it was not what he meant.

"Even faster? Under five minutes? That's pretty fast."

Matt sensed the people in line behind him. He began to sweat under his arms and fidget. Then he felt it was too late to change.

"Yeah," he said. "That'd be about right."

The woman looked at him skeptically, but wrote his name down anyway.

As it approached ten o'clock, the sounds in the Dome became different. Some runners jogged on the track. Others sat on the floor, legs stretched before them. Some laughed, some talked loudly. Some, Matt noticed, sat alone, fidgeting.

"One hundred metres, first call," bellowed a man in a white sweater with a Canadian Legion crest on it. "One hundred metres, first call. All runners in all heats of the 100 metres at the south end of the Dome. South end of the Dome."

Some runners began to move now with purpose. They were all ages and sizes: old, young, skinny, well-muscled, boys, girls, men, women.

The Royal Canadian Legion Branch #43 Track Club January All-Comers Track Meet had begun.

***

When the race officials called the runners for the 1500-metre races, Matt, Baz, and Ryan joined about twenty runners in the muster area.

"We could put these all in two heats," said the official, ticking off names from a list on his clipboard. "Nine, ten in each."

He did a quick head count. When he got to Ryan, he stopped and gazed at Ryan's orange, gelled hair.

"You. Son. You in the right place?"

"Fifteen hundred," Ryan replied.

"Hmm. Name?"

"Ryan Abolins…"

"Oh, yes, here you are. Okay. First heat. Baz Amin?"

"Here," said Baz, quietly.

"Same heat. Stick with your friend. Thompson? Matt Thompson?"

Matt pushed forward.

"That's me!" he said.

"Okay, hmm. Under five?"

"Umm," replied Matt.

"You're sure?"

Matt nodded.

The official gave him a top-to-bottom look, shrugged, and turned away. "Okay, that's the second heat."

Minutes later, Ryan and Baz were called to the start line.

The starting official lined them up at the top of the right-hand straightaway.

"Okay," she said. "Standing start. No crouching, no blocks. This is 1500 metres. Over on the far side of the track is the finish line." She indicated a place directly opposite them on the track. Several people huddled with stopwatches.

"You start here on my signal," she continued. "Once you get to the finish line over there it's six more full laps. Got that?"

Matt watched the runners. Ryan stood out. The runners were of all ages. Three looked older than his parents. One might be the age of his grandparents. Two were girls from a high school club. Two others were women about his mother's age.

"Mark!" called the starting official. She held up one hand.

"Go!" The hand came down. The runners were off.

Matt watched Ryan and Baz jostle for position on the first lap. By the time the runners came by at the end of the first lap, though, most were spread out single file. At one point, Baz led, then Ryan surged by him to lead for two full laps. But with two laps to go, three of the older runners, including one woman, cruised by them, leaving both struggling toward the finish line.

Matt was beginning to worry that he had made a mistake. The fast heat? What was he thinking?

The last of the slower runners in the heat had not yet finished when the race official called Matt's heat to the start line: five high school runners, two men the age of Matt's father, and one woman who looked to Matt to be a million years old.

He should have entered a slower heat. Now it was too late. And both Ashley and Joe Calder were watching.

5

The Heat Is On

G o!"

Avoiding elbows, Matt surged down the straightaway, already half a step behind two older runners. Ahead of him, five faster, fitter high school runners powered on.

"Go, Matt, Go!" yelled Ryan from behind the netting in the tennis court. "Show smoke."

Matt smiled back grimly.

For the first lap, he held his place in the middle of the pack. He felt strong, almost floating. From the corner of his eye he could see Ashley at trackside, her back turned, talking to someone.

They passed the finish line. One official called out the time.

"Twenty-nine, thirty, thirty-one, thirty-two... "

"Six laps! Six laps to go!" called out another official. "Looking good, looking good."

"Okay?" asked the old man beside him.

"Too fast," grunted the other older runner just ahead of Matt.

"Forty-three second laps," said the first.

"Ouch!" said the other.

Matt felt he could run faster, but was not about to say so. He glanced over his shoulder at the top of the curve. Behind him, the one woman plugged along, ten metres back. In the second lap Matt settled in, running faster then he ever had before.

Again they came up to the finish line.

"Five laps to go!" yelled an official.

"One thirteen, one fourteen, one fifteen," said another, stop-watch in hand.

"Too, too, fast," said one older runner.

"Too late, too late," said the other.

Matt wondered how they could talk while racing. He had no breath for talk.

The high school runners had surged ahead. Matt had no hope of catching them. He wondered if he'd ever be able to run that fast. At the moment, keeping up with people the age of his parents and grandparents was a challenge. The race broke into two groups: a pack of four racers from the Riders, high school seniors all of them; and Matt, the two older men, and at the back, one woman.

They started down the back straight of the third lap. Matt eased to the outside to go around the two men ahead of him.

"Don't ... hurry," said one of the men.

"First race?" asked the other.

"Cross-country," said Matt, but that's all he could say. His breath suddenly began to come in deeper gasps.

"Stay a lap," said one man. "Then see."

Matt slipped into the inside lane between the two men. Forty-three second laps! The time surprised him. In the sessions with Ms. Wellesley they had run sixty-second laps. Even then, with a rest interval between, the last couple of laps were not so easy.

Forty-three seconds!

Matt tried the math in his head. Six and three-quarters laps. At sixty seconds that would be ... he wasn't sure, it wasn't so easy to think now. They came off the bottom bend and up the straight.

"Four! Four laps to go!" called the finish-line official.

"One fifty-six, one fifty-seven, one…" Matt heard the timer's voice, but the numbers now meant nothing to him, nothing at all.

The dry air burned in his lungs. Let's see, 6.75 laps at one minute a lap. He knew the answer was near, he'd get it.

Again around the bend, up the straight. Suddenly the fun had disappeared.

"Three! Three laps to go!"

"Two forty, two forty-one, two…"

Matt glanced to the other side of the track. The high school runners were now three quarters of a lap ahead. Now the older runners began to move ahead of him, slowly but surely pulling away.

"Two! Two laps to go"

Somewhere on the back straight the grandmother trotted by him, looking easy in her stride, jogging along on a track reserved for young people. But try as he might, Matt could not keep up to her pace. She, too, continued to speed away on him.

"Way to go! Big finish!" yelled someone from the sidelines.

Ding-a-ling!

The bell sounded for the last lap — not for Matt, but for the high school runners.

Matt had lost all track of time, of pace, of speed. He had long ago given up on the idea of racing. The two older runners were now far enough ahead that he could not see them round the bend. The grandmother disappeared, too. How could they find fresh speed now?

Matt's lungs burned. His legs felt heavy. With each breath he sucked air like a fish on shore.

"Come on!" someone from the side of the track. "Don't fall back! Stay with them! Don't lose contact!"

Matt shook his head once, meaning, "No!"

He grunted once. With a sucking sigh he pulled up on his toes to surge. But instead of speed, he felt pain. Each step took all his effort. There was nothing he wanted more than to stop, to rest, to not run.

Behind him Matt could feel the high school runners, now pounding hard toward the finish line. He could be lapped! From a corner of his eye he could make out Joe Calder. Beyond that, somewhere, Ashley's face peeked through the crowd.

He pushed hard now on the straight, determined not to be lapped.

Ding-a-ling! Ding-a-ling!

The bell seemed to call him names. The official pointed him further down the track. "One lap! One lap to go!"

Someone called the time but it meant nothing to him. He wanted nothing more than to stop. Everything hurt. Behind him he could hear the crowd cheering for the high school runners as they finished. Down the back straight he glimpsed, briefly, the two male runners; behind them, the older woman. But they were long gone. He felt alone on the track. No one paid attention. With the winners now finished, people drifted onto the track.

"Track!" yelled a voice, and Matt saw Joe Calder reach forward to pull a spectator out of his path.

He carried on. Step, step, step. Each step took his full effort.

He came off the last corner and everything changed. He saw the faces. People — other runners — applauded. A cheer went up, and suddenly Matt felt strong.

Tony slapped his hands together, his leather voice loud above the others.

"Attaboy, Matt! Big finish!"

He had no reserves left for any big finish. But two more faces he did see, Joe Calder's and Ashley's, helped him pump his arms and lift legs so that he did not fade too badly.

He lunged to the finish in a run that was no longer a run.

"Five-oh-two, five-oh-three, five-oh-four…" called the official timer, still standing at the start line to give the time of completed laps. Matt crossed the line. He sucked in air. His lungs burned. The dry air of the Dome made his mouth numb. He tried to talk, but the words came out slurred.

"I nidn't wo it wus fo sast."

"Take it easy, walk it off," said Ms. Wellesley. "Get a drink."

She handed him a water bottle. Matt swished his mouth and drank.

"Good race, Matt."

Matt made a face. "Last," was all he could say. "Last."

When he had gained enough breath to look around, all he could see was Ashley watching the laughing group of high school runners.

"Five minutes and two seconds," Baz said. "Five-oh-two. That's good. You could have won our heat with that time."

Matt knew Baz was just trying to make him feel better. He felt ashamed. It would have been better to place well in a slower heat, he thought, than last in any heat.

Joe Calder fussed in a huddle with the high school runners.

Ashley was now nowhere in sight.

6

Cathy-Marie's Choice

On the following Monday, Cathy-Marie came home from school with her university application form.

"You've missed the deadline," her father said, flipping the form from front to back as though he could not decide which he should read. "You were supposed to have this in by January 12."

Cathy-Marie rolled her eyes. "I submitted it a long time ago," she said. "I did that online, back in October."

Her father shrugged. "Then what are we looking at?" He handed the form back and turned back to the package of hamburger on the kitchen counter.

"If you have applied, is there a problem we should deal with?" asked her mother, her hands full with the day's mail.

Cathy-Marie shook her head until her hair frizzed. "Choices," she said. "If I'm going to university, I'm going to do it right. I have only two weeks now to make any changes to this application."

"Oh, two weeks then," said her father. He ran a hand through his thinning brown hair. He was staring at the package of frozen meat as though his gaze alone could thaw it.

"Couldn't this wait?" asked Mrs. Thompson, ripping open one particular envelope.

"The world is not made for those who wait," said Cathy-Marie. "Not any more, anyway. We must seize the day!"

"How do you say that in Latin?" asked Mr. Thompson. "Where's the garlic salt?"

"*Carpe diem*," replied Cathy-Marie.

"There's a dime on the carpet?" said Mr. Thompson. "Where?"

"Not hamburgers again!" said Matt. "Can't you do something creative, like meat loaf?"

"Good selection, but it takes too long. Hamburgers are quicker. Now quit complaining or I'll ask your mother to cook them."

Mrs. Thompson gave her husband a tap on the forearm with a fistful of mail.

"If Matt wanted hockey pucks, he'd ask for them," she said. "I didn't get the Hartmore contract," she said.

"You are the most aggravating, annoying, pusillanimous, prevaricating family anyone ever had!" said Cathy-Marie.

"Know any more big words, Big Sister?" asked Matt.

"Don't argue," Mrs. Thompson said.

"When they turned you down, did the Hartmore people say why?" asked Mr. Thompson.

"Just that I made the short list, but they picked someone else. That's life in the PR business."

"Rhinoceros," said Cathy-Marie. "Hippopotamus. Those are two big words. Want me to look up their meanings for you?"

"Trust you to know the right words for 'big hips,'" Matt replied.

Cathy-Marie lunged at him. Had Matt not been a trained athlete, she might have caught him.

"Enough," said Mr. Thompson.

"When she's away at university next year," said Matt, from

a safe distance, "can we rent her room to someone normal?"

"Maybe we made the wrong choice last summer," said Mrs. Thompson. "Coming here. You still work too many hours. And I don't work enough. I'm down to two clients."

"It'll work out," said Mr. Thompson. "You'll see."

"Six months," said Mrs. Thompson. "You'd think things would shape up in six months." She took Cathy-Marie's form from her husband and read it quickly.

"So you've applied to five universities," she said to her daughter.

"Queen's, Western, U of T, UOIT, and Trent," said Cathy-Marie.

"So what do you want to change?" asked Mr. Thompson, retrieving the ground beef after defrosting it in the microwave.

"I don't really know," said Cathy-Marie. "I just wondered if you two had any ideas."

"I have an idea," said Matt.

"If you had an idea it would die of starvation," said Cathy-Marie.

"Speaking of starvation, you could use some," said Matt. He'd made the remark out of spite. He knew that like many teenage girls, Cathy-Marie hated any hint that she was over-weight, even though she was not. In fact, she tended, like Matt, to be thin.

"Make him stop," said Cathy-Marie, "before I prepare his head cavity for Halloween."

"Did she just call me a jack-o'-lantern?" asked Matt.

"I think she just threatened you," said Mr. Thompson. "Maybe that's a sign you'd better stop."

"So your first choice is still Queen's. Drama and English."
Cathy-Marie nodded.

"And second choice: U of T, Old English."

Her father stared at her.

"And third choice: Western, English."

Her mother stared at her.

"Let me get this straight," Mr. Thompson said. "These are the choices you made last October."

"Right."

"And you haven't changed any of them?"

"No."

"So what's this all about?"

Cathy-Marie stood with the backs of her hands on her hips. "In case I *might* want to change," she said. "This is the last chance. Some people's parents help them through the tough choices in life. But me? Oh, no."

"Tell me again," said Mr. Thompson. "Why not UOIT?" The initials stood for the University of Ontario Institute of Technology, a new university opened in 2002 in Oshawa. "You could stay here at home and save the cost of residence."

Cathy-Marie harrumphed impatiently. "If they had an English program, I would. But they don't, so I can't."

"I'm glad I don't have to choose which high school I want next year," said Matt. "Good old Courtice Secondary School. That's where I'm going."

"Good for you," said Cathy-Marie. "Grade Nine will be such an intellectual challenge for you." She said it sarcastically, as an insult, but Matt was not insulted. He looked forward to high school.

"Now, children."

"Why don't you just go back to your boring books?" asked Matt. "*King Arthur*." He spat out the term as though it tasted bad.

"And why don't you go back to your dumb computer games?" asked Cathy-Marie.

Cathy-Marie grabbed her university application form from her mother and stormed from the room. Matt and his parents stood in silence for a moment. The only sound in the kitchen was the frying of hamburgers.

"Pity that youth is wasted on young people," said Mr. Thompson. Louder, for Cathy-Marie to hear stomping her way up stairs, he added: "Mark Twain said that. In 1879."

From the upstairs landing, Cathy-Marie poked her head out from her room.

"Get it right," she said. "It's George Bernard Shaw. 'Youth is a wonderful thing. What a crime to waste it on children.'" She retreated to her room, slamming the door.

"Or something like that," said Mr. Thompson.

7

Bad Things Happen

Tony Tuchuk, the custodian at S.T. Lovey Public School, sat under the huge sink in the janitor's closet. His tool box sat beside him. Two large pipe wrenches were on his lap.

"*Snigglehalfascarpendorf*," he said.

"If I said that, I'd have to stay after school," said Matt Thompson. He had been sent by Ms. Wellesley to ask the janitor something important that he could not now remember.

"Or warsh your mouth out with soap," said Tony, a small man with wiry sinews in his arms instead of muscles. "Without a doubt, with soap." He pronounced the words crisply with an English accent. Matt wondered where he had found the "r" in the word *wash*.

Matt had first met Tony the day before he had started at S.T. Lovey — the same day Gavin Richards had tricked him into climbing onto the roof of a portable. He didn't know it then, but Tony had become a supporter. He was very quiet, but affable. Everybody in the school knew him, and he was everyone's friend.

The sink under which had had ducked his head overflowed with soapy, grey water. He tightened the grip of the wrench to open the sink trap.

"So what's your teacher want?" he asked from under the sink.

"How'd you know Ms. Wellesley wanted you?"

"She sent you. Teachers send students to find me only when they need something. That's my job. So what is it?"

"Somebody dropped a jar of orange juice," Matt replied, "She needs a clean-up."

"Stone the crows." Tony's English accent was crisp, with rounded "O's", so the word "stone" sounded more like "stown". "Cleanup in aisle five. Be right down. Hand me that bucket, will you?" he asked Matt.

Matt handed him the pail, which the custodian slid under the S-shaped sink trap.

"You know what that does, don't you?" he asked.

"What? The sink?" asked Matt. "You use that to pour the water used to scrub the floor."

"If you didn't know what a sink did you'd be in bad shape for the eighth grade," said Tony. "No, the trap under the sink. This S-shaped part here."

"Traps stuff, doesn't it? Isn't that why they call it a trap?"

"Partly. It's this shape so that water always sits in it. That stops the gases from coming back up the drain."

"Gases?"

"Otherwise, the sink wouldn't smell nice at all," said Mr. Tony. He jerked on the wrench until the nutcap gave freely. Then he unscrewed the cap with his fingers.

"But the trap also gets clogged up with soap scum, and dirt, and anything else that you little urchins decide to put down the sink," he said. "And whatever else just happens."

He didn't smile. But his eyes twinkled.

"Ah! There were are!"

A gob of black slime oozed from the hole at the bottom of the trap and dropped into the bucket. With a big slurp, the contents of the sink followed.

Tony carefully edged his fingers into the bottom of trap. He pulled out some gum foil and two marbles.

"Amazing how this junk gathers," he said.

Matt wondered about a man like Tony. He was old — he must be fifty at least, Matt thought. The top of his head was bald. Thin hair traced a path along the side of his head above each ear, making him look something like a sad-sack clown.

"That was a pretty good run you did the other day," Tony said, only his feet visible from under the sink, breaking what seemed to Matt to have been a long silence.

Matt shrugged.

"You not satisfied?" said the older man.

After his race at the all-comers meet, Matt had been discouraged, and tired. He had napped on the tennis courts on the infield that afternoon, using his running bag for a pillow. He hadn't paid attention to any of the other races. He hadn't wanted to.

"Came last," Matt said finally.

"Turn on the cold water for me, would you?" asked Tony, still on his back under the sink. He placed the bucket back under the drain. "Let's see if we can get this rinsed out right."

Matt turned on the tap. The cold water ran into the sink and out into the bucket again.

"That works well," said the custodian. "Hold it a minute."

Another pause, and then he said: "Last in a fast heat like that isn't bad, you know. You almost broke five minutes."

Matt recognized the tone. He'd gotten it from his friends. "You did well, you beat my time, blather, blather, blather." They hadn't been out there, running that last lap, in last place, all alone so everyone could see. Behind somebody's grandmother.

"That doesn't matter."

Tony didn't say anything just then. Matt watched as his grime-blackened fingers screwed the access cap back on the trap.

"Try it again."

Matt again turned on the tap. The water whirled down the sink and disappeared.

The janitor began gathering up his tools, placing them neatly into his tool box.

"Tony of all trades," he said. "Gardener, plumber, carpenter, cleaner." He whistled something tuneless. Then, before Matt could leave, he said, "Baz said you're wanting to join Joe Calder and the Durham Riders."

"I didn't say that. That is, I never told Baz."

"Some things you don't have to say," said Mr. tuchuk. "But people pick up the muddle of hints and put the puzzle together. Word travels fast in the forest."

"Ms. Wellesley tell you?"

"No, actually, she didn't. But we runners, we're different. Because we're different, we stick together. I hear stuff."

"I didn't know you were a runner," Matt said. "Even at the track, I didn't see you running."

"Runner? I plod along now and then. People my age, we're lucky to keep moving. We make good cheerleaders." He smiled, then continued. "Calder's pretty focused on competition."

Matt leaned over the sink and watched Tony at work.

"I've…" he faltered, then continued. "I used to want to play hockey more than anything," he said. "But since I started here, I've found I like running. I'd love to be a member of the Riders. But after that horrid all-comers meet, I don't stand a chance."

"One race isn't a career."

"Yeah, but I sucked, Tony. Big time."

"Let me ask you a question," Tony said, stopping his work and looking Matt directly in the eye.

"Would you go in that same heat again?"

"The under-five? No way. I've learned my lesson."

Tony gathered his tools and placed them in his tool box. "Cocky isn't bad," he said, his English accent showing through more than usual. "And you should learn something from each race."

"Joe'll never look at me now," said Matt.

Tony looked at Matt sharply. "Don't be so sure. Joe knew what was coming. He knew what you'd look like those last three laps."

"He did?"

"Matt, there was only one person at the Dome last Saturday who didn't know you'd entered a heat that was too fast for you. Everybody but that one person knew you'd crash and burn."

"Me?"

"Well, maybe two. That Grovier girl seemed to think you were a hero. Anyway, you catch on quick. Now, if you think back, a lot of people probably tried to tell you you weren't ready for a heat that fast."

Matt thought that over for a moment.

"The lady who took registration. The old guy I ran with, Ms. Wellesley..." Matt now recognized the hints people had tried to give him.

"Now, if they'd told you not to go in that heat, they'd have been wrong," said Tony. "You've always got to be ready to challenge yourself. To see how far you can stretch."

"What I really want is to join the Riders when I'm in high school."

"So," said Tony. "What are you doing to make that happen?"

"What do you mean?"

"If you dream about stuff happening you can dream your life away," said Tony. "Dream, dream, dream. To make it come true, you have to do something."

"I'm running. Every Tuesday and Thursday, I'm running.

Well, I was. Now that Ms. Wellesley can't coach us, I don't know."

"Two days a week. That's a good start. What about the other five days?"

"Run every day?"

"Sooner or later. And why the Riders. Why not join the Clarington Vikings?"

"The Vikings?" Matt asked. "Never heard of them."

"Well," said Tony, picking up his tool box. "Find out. They have an excellent coach. They're nearby. You'd be able to continue running now and all summer, and be ready for cross-country at Courtice Secondary next fall."

Matt said: "Vikings?"

"Think about it," said Tony. "But I'd better get down there and clean up the orange juice before the bell rings and everybody's tramping through it and tracking their sticky feet everywhere. If you don't deal with stuff when it happens, it only gets worse."

Matt wondered why Tony would think he would join the Vikings — a club he had never heard of, with members he'd never met. It certainly did not sound like a track club that would impress Ashley.

The recess bell rang, and all of a sudden they were in the middle of a rush of students bumping each other to get outside for recess. He didn't get a chance to ask anything more.

8

Mud Pies

Matt met Ashley beside the kindergarten compound by accident one Thursday after school in the first week in March. It was an unusually mild day, the sun warming his face. Most of the snow had gone, leaving puddles and dirty, stranded mini icebergs where it had been piled from parking lots and sidewalks. Two first-graders crouched near the fence, stomping a puddle and turning the resutling soupy mud into mud pies.

"You skip track?" asked Matt, when he first saw Ashley,and knew he would be unable to avoid her.

"Well, duh," replied Ashley.

"Me, too," said Matt, realizing he was repeating the obvious.

The previous two weeks had not been happy for Matt. Nor, for that matter, for any of the other S.T. Lovey runners. Since Ms. Wellesley stopped coaching, several of them had continued to run at the Dome, every Tuesday and Thursday. But it wasn't the same.

First of all, Ms. Wellesley wasn't there. Well, sometimes she was. But now she would just run on her own. She would speak to them only to say "Hello" or "Bye now!" and her challenging workouts were a thing of the past.

"I'll go tomorrow," said Matt. "Or maybe Saturday. It doesn't matter much anymore."

Ashley snapped her bubble gum as Baz came around the corner.

"You, too, huh?" said Matt.

They formed a trio, shuffling aimlessly toward the back of the school, headed for the park. Matt tried to think of something to say, but couldn't.

At the corner of the school they met Gavin. Kathryn came up the path from the park.

"Looks like we're all here," said Ashley.

"Isn't anybody at the Dome?" asked Baz.

Kathryn looked up. "Well, I have an excuse," she said. "I've got to go to the barns." In addition to running, Kathryn owned a horse, which she kept at a stable near Bowmanville. She'd missed many days at the track because of the horse.

"I had to stay in after school," said Gavin.

"Ryan went," Kathryn said.

"I thought he quit," said Baz. "Ryan gets to the Dome and none of us are there, he will quit. Besides, hasn't he still got that bad leg?"

"And that temper of his," said Ashley. "I mean, like, remember the fuss he made last fall over Mattie?"

"Mattie?" asked Kathryn, raising one eyebrow and shifting her gaze quickly from Ashley to Matt.

"Matt," corrected Ashley. "But is his father still, like, going to sue the school over him kicking in the door and all?"

Baz dismissed that idea. "Naw, it'd never happen. My dad says his dad is just like a big whale, spraying from the blowhole."

"But somebody from the school board must have heard that," said Matt. "That could be why they got tough with Ms. Wellesley."

The group of friends drifted across the mostly deserted schoolyard toward the park. From time to time, Gavin would break away, running, bouncing before turning and hopping on one foot, backwards so he could still see everyone. But mostly they drifted, like a single-celled creature that could not think, but only drift toward a sunshine for which it had no name.

"So what do we do?" asked Kathryn, finally, after a particularly heavy silence.

"What do you mean?" asked Baz. "What is there to do? I mean, Ms. Wellesley isn't going to coach us. Not until spring, when we can run outdoors again."

"Like, duh, *today* she means," said Ashley. "We could all be running outdoors *today*."

"Who wants to run anyway?" asked Matt.

"I mean when Ms. Wellesley can start up the 100-Kilometre Club again," said Baz. "Mrs. MacMillan said we could do that."

"Yeah, on school property," said Kathryn. "Think how much fun that's going to be. It's bad enough running around the park on our field day. Running laps on a rough field? I don't think so."

Somehow the group had continued across the schoolyard circling always to the left, ending up almost where they had started, behind Portable One. It was about this point that Matt got an idea.

"There are things we can do," he said, quietly.

"Yeah, like what?" asked Baz. "Wait for May?"

"Look," said Matt. "We all wanted to run so we'll have an advantage in track and field this year, right? Wasn't that what we were doing?"

Kathryn and Ashley nodded. Baz shrugged.

"Okay, we can join other clubs. I mean, if we're serious."

Baz looked at the two girls and turned to Gavin, who was stomping on a puddle nearby.

"He's serious," Baz said, with a smile, cocking his thumb toward Matt.

"No, no, listen." Matt spread his hands out in front of him. "The other day Tony said… "

"Who's Tony?" interrupted Kathryn.

"Mr. Tuchuk. Our custodian. He said there were other clubs. We could join them. Like the Vikings."

"The Vikings?"

"A track club in Clarington. Not as good as the Riders, but Tony…"

"Or we could ask Joe Calder if we could join the Riders," said Baz. "Yeah, right. 'Joe, we're a bunch of whiners, and we want to join your club and go to the Olympics!'"

"All Joe's athletes have to go to Dwyer High School," said Ashley. "I heard somebody at the track say that. So he can coach them at school and at track. I mean, who would want to do that?"

"With twice-a-day workouts," said Kathryn.

"And track meets almost every weekend."

"Those guys are cute," said Ashley.

"There are girls in that club, too," said Kathryn. "Or hadn't you noticed? Ms. Wellesley used to run for them. I heard she might again."

"You have to be good to run in that club," said Baz. "That's the main point."

"Matt's probably good enough," said Kathryn. "You, too, Baz. But I don't think…"

For a fleeting moment, Matt thought he'd had a brilliant idea. But like many brilliant ideas, this one sparked once, like a shooting star, and then disappeared into the murky background of the Milky Way.

It was Ashley who came up with a plan that could work.

9

Ashley's Idea

A shley arrived at school on Tuesday of the following week in a funk, slammed her locker door shut, and turned on Matt. There was anger in her voice.

"Kathryn said that Baz told her that Ryan said you wanted to join the Riders."

Matt was surprised that Ashley knew this fact and by the route by which she had learned it. Rather than react, he shrugged, as much as to say, "It's no big deal."

"I never thought you'd abandon your friends like that," she said. "Ever. *If* you did, I'd never speak to you again!"

Matt floundered. "I never said I wanted to join any dumb club," he replied. "I never said that. To Ryan. To Baz. And certainly never to Kathryn."

"You're not good enough, anyway," said Ashley. "You have to be *really* good to join the Riders. Like Ms. Wellesley. She used to be a member of the Riders. She used to be one of top ten distance runners in Canada."

"I mean, who didn't know that?" said Robert Maxwell, who had just happened to pass by. "She went to university in the States on a track scholarship. She could make it to the Olympics maybe if she had time to train properly."

"Been reading again, Robert?" asked Ashley. "Someday your eyeballs are going to fall out from overuse. Is there anything you don't know?"

Robert smiled bashfully, but said, "If there is, it isn't worth knowing." Robert had run cross-country the previous fall, but had chosen not to train with the others at the Dome.

"Well, she might have more time to train now since she doesn't have to coach us," said Matt.

"*Can't* coach us," said Ashley. "There is a difference."

"Big deal. Can't. Won't. What's the difference?"

Ashley stuck out her lower lip and glowered at Matt. "*Hello*, is Matt still around? The difference is, Mr. Runner, that she coached us at the Dome when she didn't have to. After school. On her own time. So she's not the one you should be mad at."

Matt, surprised by Ashley's anger, took two small steps backward and found himself against his own open locker door.

"Okay, okay, okay, okay," he said.

"Furthermore, instead of feeling sorry for ourselves, we should be helping Ms. Wellesley," Ashley added. "She's an awesome runner. She's always telling us we should be all that we can be. I think she should, too."

"Well, I ..." Matt stumbled over the words.

"That is, instead of just worrying about ourselves and trying to join the Riders or something like that. Ms. Wellesley should be the best runner she can be. Don't you think so, Mattie?"

At this point Matt was flummoxed. "Sure ... yes, why not ... I, um, think."

Ashley slammed her locker door shut and snapped the lock into place. "What you think is not important," she said, turning on one heel before heading toward the classroom. "What counts is what we do about it. And we definitely have to do something."

When he thought about it later, Matt realized he had just

witnessed the birth and formation of a plan, all within two minutes, in the hallway of S.T. Lovey Elementary School.

By afternoon recess, that thought had grown to become common knowledge in the 100-Kilometre Club. And by the time the bell had rung at the end of the school day, that one idea had become the entire focus of the runners. And Matt found himself standing by his locker facing a determined Ashley.

"Go ahead," she said. "You ask her."

"Me?" asked Matt. He had half retreated into his locker. Ashley kept a finger pointed directly at his chest.

"Yes, you," she said. "You're the ideal one. If I ask her, she'll think…"

"But I don't really know what this is all about," said Matt. "*You* ask her. And what are you going to say. 'Excuse me, Ms. Wellesley, if you're not going to coach us, then who is?' Is that what I'm supposed to say?"

"Just ask her if she's going to join the Riders," said Baz.

Matt looked from Baz, to Ashley, to Kathryn.

"It's your idea, Ash," he said. "Why don't you ask her?"

Matt had turned toward his locker and did not see the downcast eyes and shuffling feet that came next. He did hear the voice behind him:

"Ask her what?" said Ms. Wellesley.

"Ask Ms. Wellesley if…" Matt half turned, saw who he was talking to, and faltered.

"Ask me what?" repeated the teacher.

"Ask… if …" Matt's mind spun like a bicycle with a broken chain.

Ms. Wellesley stood a half-step too close to Matt, and made no attempt to move.

"You'll never get a better chance to ask."

Matt felt abandoned. The others had turned, heads hidden in

their lockers to avoid eye contact. Robert slipped quietly away. Ashley did a little *hum-dee-hum* as she tossed her backpack over one shoulder, shook her hair free of her collar, and began tiptoeing for the door.

"Well?"

Matt realized he was on his own now. He pulled himself back out of his locker.

"It wasn't me," he said. "It was … we, that is, wanted to know if you were going to run with the Riders now."

Before she disappeared around the corner, Ashley leaned back and firmly stuck her tongue out at him. Her back was to Ashley, so Ms. Wellesley continued.

"With the Riders?" said Ms. Wellesley. "Funny you should ask. I've thought of it. But my first aim is to deal with my promise to you guys" She said it like that, as though she were a person, Matt thought, and not just a teacher. "I promised to coach you this term. I'm still looking for a way to make that happen."

"But you…"

"But, but, but, but. You sound like a motorboat, Matt," said the teacher. "This ban by the school board was not what we needed. But we don't just give up. We deal with it. Just in case the others ask, I'm still running. And Joe has asked if I'm ready to get back into heavy training. And the answer is, yes, I think I'm ready. But first I have a commitment to the 100-Kilometre Club."

She left him in the hallway, his mouth gaping like a guppy out of water. He was slowly getting the idea that joining the Riders might *not* be the best way to impress Ashley.

Just before Ms. Wellesley disappeared into her office, she turned to Matt.

"And next time Ashley has a bright idea, maybe she should do the talking."

10

Coach's Corner

Joe Calder placed the back of his wrists on each hip. His clipboard dangled, pinched between the thumb and forefinger of his left hand.

"Before you begin, the answer is no," he said.

He stood at the side of the track at the Oshawa Civic Dome. Tennis balls thunked. Runners cruised by on the track. Baz and Kathryn watched, a discreet distance away.

"But we haven't even…" Matt tried to form words, but they would not come. He looked to Ashley for help, but Ashley looked more like Bambi, helpless and caught in a thicket.

"I know you haven't," said Joe. "And I'd like to be more accommodating. But I am a busy man, and I've heard it all before. Let me see. You'd like to join the Riders, right?"

"Yeah, well…"

"You and twenty-four others. No, make that 124 others. It just can't happen. I have room for only so many athletes, and each of those is carefully chosen."

Joe looked down at both Matt and Ashley. At six foot two, Joe looked down on most people. It made Matt feel small and powerless, as though he was still in kindergarten.

"You know why, do you not?"

Matt shrugged. "We're not good enough?"

Joe shook his head from side to side. "*Yet*," he said, adding a word to Matt's sentence. "Always add that additional word, 'yet.' You're not good enough. Yet. To be good enough, you first have to believe you will be. Now, you, Matt. Back at the all-comer's meet a few weeks ago. You were in over your head, but you didn't give up. I like that. You ran a good race. Keep doing that and you will do well."

A light came on in Ashley's eyes. "But we need a coach." She said this with conviction, like it really meant something.

"No, young lady. You *want* a coach," Joe smiled tiredly. "There is a world of difference. I don't coach people until they have shown, by performance, that they have both the talent and the drive to benefit from my training. Period. No exceptions."

"But our coach has been told she can't coach us," Matt said. "The school board said it would fire her." He didn't know if this last part was really true, but it sounded good.

"That's crazy," Joe said. This country has enough trouble getting people to exercise and stay fit without stupidity like that. Look, all you need is someone to give you running times and all that — someone to encourage you, get you to enjoy running. That's not my job. I'm a national-level coach. The athletes I train are either national level or close to it, with a chance of becoming the best. It is not an efficient use of my time to coach people who haven't first displayed the talent and desire needed at the national level. That's why the answer is no."

"What would we have to do?" asked Ashley.

"First you have to run. A lot. Have fun running. Run every day. Not just here, indoors, if available, outdoors, whenever you can. Get an adult involved if you can, but that's not necessary. When I was a kid, we just got together and did things on our own. You can still do that. Run, enter track meets, get experience. You get your times down and show progress. Win your events in your elementary school events. Do that, and maybe I could take a look by the time you're in high school, maybe Grade Ten, Eleven. "

"That's what we're trying to do, Mr. Calder," said Matt. "But the board of education won't let our teacher coach us anymore. Here. During the winter."

"Please, call me Joe. If you're at the school where I teach, then you can call me Mr. Calder. Who was your coach?"

"Ms. Wellesley," said Ashley.

"Fran Wellesley? If she's as good a coach as she is a runner, then you have a dandy. You said the board won't allow it?"

"Something about insurance," said Ashley. "They ripped out a playground, too."

"Oh, boy. It figures. Lawyers, eh? Yeah, great. So you need a coach. There are a lot of other runners who need coaches. I wish I could help you, I really do. But why not try the Oshawa Legion club? Or the Clarington Vikings? They're both good clubs, have good coaches. They'll give you good workouts and get you out to meets and stuff. That's all you really need now. "

Matt knew that Joe was making sense, but the answer didn't fit.

"We just need someone to do what Ms. Wellesley was doing," said Ashley. "For a couple of months. So we can get ready for track season. That's all. If you could just…"

Joe lifted one hand, slowly. "Whoa, hold up there, miss. I know what you're saying. I've seen what Fran was doing with you. There were what, five, six of you…"

"Seven, actually, when we're all here," said Matt.

"Okay seven," said Joe. "But Fran kept you coming, kept you focused, right? And now that she can't do it officially, you're losing focus. People don't show up, don't know what to do when they do."

"That pretty well sums it up," Matt replied.

Joe gave a half-chuckle, the type of laugh people sometimes give when something is strange but not really funny.

"You know," said Joe, "Fran used to train with me."

"We know," said Ashley. "She's good."

"You don't know the half of it," said Joe. "She's national level now — or was, back in August before she hurt her ankle. So she's lost something. But she's got talent. I'd love to get her back training."

Ashley bounced twice on both feet.

"She is training," she said. "She runs every day now. And she is good."

"She's running, but she's not training," Joe corrected. "To get to a competitive level she has to be training. That's more than just running. Training also means having a serious coach that you will listen to. Back in the fall, she thought she was ready again. But before I could get her back on the track to train, she ran that damned cross-country run at High Park."

"But she came first in that!" said Ashley.

"She may have come first, but she did too much on an ankle that hadn't fully mended. A good coach would have told her that. I could have told her that. Oh, well. But running is good. Now, maybe if she's not trying to coach you guys, we could get her back on track."

Matt saw the look in Ashley's eyes. He had the same idea.

"We could get her back," he blurted.

"What?" Joe replied, surprised.

"It's true, Joe," said Ashley. "We could get her back to training with you. She wants to. But she told Matt there was just one thing that was holding her back."

"What's that?"

"Us."

"Beg pardon?" said Joe, cocking an ear toward Matt.

"Us," said Matt. "She's ready to rejoin you and the Riders. But first she wants to make sure we have a coach."

Ashley and Matt fell silent while Joe ran a thumb under his lower lip.

"She would start training again if you guys had a coach?" Joe said.

"Yes," said Ashley. "She's ready to train. All she needs to do is make sure that we have a coach."

Joe laughed out loud. "A ... coach!" he said, and guffawed.

"A coach," said Matt. "Who coaches like she did. Tuesdays and Thursdays. Tell us what to do. Just ... guide us."

"For two months," added Ashley. "That's all."

"And that would get her back to training with the Riders?" Ashley and Matt nodded in unison.

Joe furrowed his brow.

"Deal," he said at last, holding out his hand first to Ashley, then to Matt. "I'll call her tonight."

11

Time Trial

Joe Calder stood with eighteen runners before him on the stretch mats at the south end of the Civic Dome.

"Time trial," he shouted.

"All right!" called out several of the older high school runners Matt admired.

"What's a time trial?" Matt asked.

Joe smiled. "Anybody want to explain to our newcomers?"

"We all run the same distance and Joe times us," said one of them. "It's like a race. Just to show Joe how you're doing."

"Oh."

"What's the distance, Joe?" asked one of the older runners.

"Three thousand metres."

Ms. Wellesley entered the far end of the Dome and walked toward them.

"She running, too?" asked Ashley. "I mean, like, are all of us running?" All of the Lovey runners, including Ms. Wellesley, had been training with the Riders for the past two weeks. Matt had watched her workouts in awe — she ran both long *and* fast, Matt concluded, although what was fast to him, he had discovered, was just a warm-up for Ms. Wellesley.

"*Everybody* runs," said Joe.

Ashley made a face. Kathryn winced. Baz shrugged.

"Except Ryan," Joe added. When the Lovey group had started "training" with the Riders, Joe had surprised everyone by insisting Ryan be included in the group. But having included Ryan, Joe then refused to allow him on the track. Instead, he had assigned Ryan his workouts in the weight room on an exercise bike. Only during the previous session had he been allowed to even jog. Even then, Joe would let him to join his friends only for warm-up and cool down.

"For this time trial, you'll do the usual warm-up, about twenty minutes easy jogging. Some strides to get the legs turning over. Then we'll be ready for it. You guys ready to win?"

"You mean, like, win, as in *win*?" asked Ashley, her jaw slack. She looked at the high school boys who were getting ready for the warm-up. "I mean, us? Against, them? You're just going to make us look stupid, right?"

"Here's how it works," said Joe. "You have to predict your finish time. We do a staggered start — the slower people off first, the faster ones later — according to the predicted time of finish."

"But that means …" said Matt, the truth dawning.

"Ah, yes, it does mean that if everybody runs the time they predict, you'll all finish together. That happens, and you'll have lots to talk about while you're cooling down."

"What do think of that, Ashes?" asked Baz.

"I think those high school guys have cute butts," replied Ashley.

After the warm-up, Joe walked among the stretching runners, asking them for their predicted finishing times. Matt doubled his 1500-metre time and added a minute: twelve-thirty. He knew he could run twelve minutes and thirty seconds. At least, he hoped.

"Tell this guy about the soft times," Joe said to Kevin Baker, one of the high school runners.

"Soft times?" asked Matt.

Kevin grinned. "You can't put down anything slower than what you ran over the same distance last time. You put in a soft time, one that you can beat easily, and you'll likely finish first. But then you'll have to buy doughnuts for those who run their predicted times."

"Donuts?" asked Baz.

"It's the only time coach says we can eat doughnuts," said Kevin. "Once a month. After the time trial. Of course, if you run too slow, you may still have to buy the donuts anyway. It works both ways. You might want to have another look at your time."

"But I ran five … thirty," Matt said, looking around to see if Ashley and Baz were listening. "In the 1500 metres back in January. And it hurt."

"And now it's the end of March. You've been training. But it's okay by me. I like mine with jelly fillings and a double-double."

Matt looked across the mats. Joe looked back and held up five fingers, plus one. Eleven minutes?

Joe thought Matt could run 3000 metres in eleven even.

Matt signalled back with a raised thumb. Fifteen seconds ahead of Baz? He didn't feel it would be that okay.

Warm-up, stretches, and strides were over. Joe signalled everybody to the start line.

"Ashley, you go first," said Joe. He stood by the start line, his clipboard cradled in the crook of his right arm, his pen poised.

"Then Kathryn, Baz, Matt. Then Mark, Noah, and Kevin." The last three were high school runners.

"What about me?" asked Ms. Wellesley. Every day at workout, she had worked on her own, completing whatever tasks Joe had set for her.

"Forgot about you, Fran," said Joe, his smile indicating he had not.

"As if anyone could forget me," said Ms. Wellesley. "I'm warmed up and ready. It sure sounds like more fun than intervals," she said.

"So what'll it be? Ten even? That would start you off just before Kevin. He's running nine-thirty."

"That's about right. I haven't tapered, so this is like a tempo run. Without a taper or anything."

"Ten minutes?" said Ashley. "Like, without stopping for coffee or anything?"

"You guys ready?" said Joe. "Ashley, Kathryn, Baz, Matt, Susan, Kevin, Harmony, Bobby, Fran, and Jake."

"So we get to play Catch Ashes," said Kevin, laughing.

"Catch Ashes and she paints your name on her pencil case," said Ryan, who jogged by.

"You jerk!" yelled Ashley. "I don't do that anymore."

"Or any less," said Ryan.

"You not running?" asked Matt.

"'Nother time, bro," said Ryan.

"He's still mending that leg," said Joe, although it didn't seem like he'd been listening.

"Perhaps you'd prefer to catch Ms. Wellesley," said Kathryn.

"It's the other way around," said Ashley. "She'll catch you, only when she does she'll throw you back."

The staggered start, with fourteen runners involved, made the time trial less tense than a race, Matt thought.

Joe started Ashley off with one spoken word:

"Now!" as he clicked his stopwatch.

***

On the 223-metre Civic Dome track, 3000 metres was thirteen-and-a-half laps, give or take a metre. They started from the southwest corner by the stretching mats, farthest from the entrance. Half a lap took them counterclockwise to the start line.

"Pacing," said Kevin.

Kevin was one of the stars of the Riders. Matt had learned he was sixteen, in Grade Eleven. He had short, dark brown hair. He was thin but well-muscled.

"This time trial. You're all out there alone," he told Matt. "In a race, or doing intervals with a partner, you key off somebody else. Here, you'll be alone. You have to learn what you can do."

"Leave the kid alone," said one of the other high school runners. "I like doughnuts too much."

Several laughed.

Out on the track, Ashley was running smoothly. From a distance, her pace looked slow. But she was passing joggers on the track, including even Ryan.

"Looks slow, doesn't it?" asked Kevin.

Matt nodded. As he watched, Kathryn caught up to Ashley about halfway around her first lap.

"Just remember, she's running about one-minute laps," said Kevin. "That's seven-minute miles. None of you guys could do that when you first started coming down here last fall."

"I didn't even know you'd noticed us," said Matt.

"Ashley's pretty hard not to notice, even for a kid in Grade Eight," said Kevin, nudging Matt with an elbow to indicate that he was just kidding.

"Watch that other girl, though," said Kevin. "She's either going to burn out in glorious flames or set a new PB."

"Kathryn. A PB?"

"Personal best."

"I'll bet on glorious flames," said Noah.

"Easy for you to say," said Kevin. "But we'll find out how much fire she has."

The runners waiting to start milled about. Ms. Wellesley moved among them. She shook her arms and legs, as though she was trying to rid herself of jitters.

"You're up next, Baz," said Joe, lifting a warning finger.

Kathryn came by in her second lap, followed by Ashley.

"Now!"

Baz fell in behind the two girls, but closed steadily, until he glided past Ashes, and then Kathryn.

"The secret is to get a strong, comfortable pace," said Kevin. "I know the first few times I did this, I would start out too fast. Figured I had to catch up all at once. Instead, you do it steadily. Look, Baz is now two laps behind Ashley, one lap behind … what's her name?"

"Kathryn."

"Yeah. Kathryn. He has to spread that two laps over thirteen or he's going to be in big trouble."

Matt remembered how he had felt completing the last few laps of the 1500 at the all-comers meet. He had started out too fast and those last laps hurt.

"You're up, Matt."

Matt waited for Joe's signal.

"Now!"

Matt surged forward and powered around the bend and up the straight. Baz had started half a minute before him. Now he ran slightly more than a half lap ahead.

Matt felt strong. Coming up the straightaway for the first half lap to the place where he would finish, he knew he could run much faster. One of the other runners not doing this trial counted down.

"Thirteen. Thirteen laps to go."

Matt rounded the top curve and started down the back straight to where he had started. Joe stood, pencil poised over his clipboard. He held a pencil, clipboard, even a stopwatch. Still, Joe somehow gave a signal that Matt understood: back off, back off.

Strange, Matt thought. It didn't feel like he was running fast.

Still, he now focused on the back of Baz's shirt, still almost half a lap ahead. What was it? Thirty seconds difference? Over thirteen laps. Two seconds a lap, plus a bit.

On the curves, he could already glance slyly behind him and see Mark, one of the high school runners, running strongly and eating up the distance between them. He could see he was gaining on Kathryn and Ashley.

Baz remained stubbornly in front.

Matt held to his pace. In his second lap, he did catch Ashley. By the end of his third lap, he'd pulled up beside Kathryn.

"Looking good," he tried to say, but the words came out as a grunt. Kathryn gave him a helpless look, something Bambi might have flashed at hunters.

Still, Baz did not let up, and he could not eat into the half lap distance between them.

"Reel 'em in."

Matt didn't hear Joe say the words as he went by, completing his fifth lap. But he saw the coach make a casting motion with a winding flick of his wrist, as though he were reeling in a fishing rod.

Reel him in?

Matt had settled nicely into his pace. At this rate, he knew he could complete the run without major pain. But behind him, Mark's footsteps grew louder.

Matt focused on holding his form. Somewhere in the eighth

lap, the run changed. Coming up the back straight toward the finish line, he was suddenly aware of Baz's back getting ever so much closer.

"Four! Four laps to go!" said the counter.

Kathryn was within sight down the back straight. But Matt hit the straight before Baz had turned the curve at the far end. The half-lap difference shrank.

Matt rose then on the balls of his feet. He pulled his strength into a toughened effort. Not one that would suck all the oxygen out of his lungs. Just enough to bring Baz closer, one metre at a time.

He could hear nothing now but relentless footsteps behind him. Mark's grunt-like breathing from behind urged him on.

"Three! Three laps to go!"

Now Baz grew closer still. He caught glimpses of Ashley somewhere half a lap or more ahead. His attention was on Baz. Twenty metres? Matt could not count. He ran, moving his arms like pistons, his legs like coiled springs. For half a lap he felt like he was floating, like a bounding gazelle. He could run like this forever.

"Two laps! Two laps to go."

He caught Baz at the top of the track just under the four-armed clock. The floating feeling left him. Within a few steps, his legs had turned to tree trunks. His arms grew heavy.

Every step now took willpower. Each step became a mechanical motion: move this leg, then the other arm, bring the left leg up, pull with the arms.

Ding-a-ling! Ding-a-ling!

From somewhere Joe had pulled out a hand bell. He stood at the finish line ringing like a town crier.

"Last lap! Last lap!"

Ahead of him, Ashley continued her strong, even pace. On

the back straight, Matt caught Kathryn, who had started too fast and was now struggling. Behind him, Mark grunted, heaved. But there were other sounds now, other steps moving closer. As he came off the last curve at the bottom of the track, he gave one last wild-eyed glance out of the corner of his eye. Mark. Kevin. Ms. Wellesley. Somebody else. All were strung out behind, all poised to sweep around him on the final straight.

He dug deep now. Toenails scraped into his shoes. Now, one last surge swept away the fatigue. Once again, he floated, free, fast, a superman of a runner.

Up the final fifty metres of the final straight he chased Ashley, the other runners strung out behind like street urchins.

"Twelve thirty! Twelve thirty-one, twelve thirty-two…"

Matt winced over the finish line, still several steps behind Ashley. Four, five, six steps he took to come to a halt. Under the dome clock he put hands on his knees and drank air, sucked in whatever his lungs could find. His chest burned. His mouth was numb and dry.

"Great run!" said Kevin, gasping up behind him.

"Twelve thirty?" gasped Matt. "I did all that for twelve thirty?"

"Relax. That was from the staggered start, remember? Ashley had a two-minute lead on all of us! Subtract that."

Ms. Wellesley pulled up, clapped him on the back.

"You ran ten thirty," she said. "I couldn't catch you! What lit your fire four laps back?"

"Huh?" said Matt, unable to say much else.

"You were coming back to me nicely all along," said Ms. Wellesley, barely breathing hard. "Then you started to pull away. I mean that. Pull away. Both you and Ashley."

"Great run, Matt!" said Baz, pulling up in gasps. Kathryn pulled up, her final steps in distress.

"Twelve fifteen!" said Ashley. "I beat my time by fifteen seconds!"

"Don't congratulate yourself too soon," said Mark with a smile. "Joe will just increase your workout. And next time he'll expect you to knock another fifteen seconds off your time."

Ashley hunched over to catch her breath. Finally, she said: "But when I'm fit … when I can do those … workouts. Then it'll be easier."

Kevin rolled his eyes.

"Relax, kid. It never gets easier. No matter how fit you get, racing feels just the same. It hurts."

"But …" Ashley seemed confused.

"All that happens when you get fitter," said Kevin with a smirk, "is that you run faster. If you're lucky, you learn to enjoy the pain of the race."

"Ouch!" said Kathryn.

"The only reward is the doughnuts. Which Matt and Ashley now owe everybody, since they both put in soft times and wiped the field! That awesome run will cost you a both a half-dozen doughnuts!"

Afterward, in the coffee shop, Ashley wiped jelly filling from the corner of her mouth and told Matt she was really proud of his run that day. Matt told her she had done well, too.

12

Finding a Fit

Ashley stood with the others beside the stage in the school gym.

"These are the uniforms?" she asked.

She held up the tops. A crest that said *S.T. Lovey Larks* was on one side. On the other was a large number 89. It was after school on a Wednesday. They were gathered around a cardboard box.

"I have, like, larger bikinis," said Ashley, holding the shirt from her shoulders. It came almost to her waist.

"Get a larger one," said Kathryn.

"This is the largest one," said Ashley.

"I *mean*, these will be perfect for the kindergarten basketball team," said Ryan.

"I should be able to find one that fits me," said Gavin.

"You're about the only one," said Ashley. "I mean, do they think we're all kids, or what?"

"I don't think these will work for track and field," said Baz. "Unless we pin them to our shirts. He held up one top over his chest so that the crest showed.

"Lovey Larks?" said Ryan. "Lovey *Larks*?"

"Well, at least we don't have to wear them next year," said Matt. "In high school, we'll have something different."

"You haven't seen the Cougars outfits, have you?" asked Kathryn. "They're not much better."

"I get to wear one," said Gavy, who had dug into the box of sweaters to find one that fit. "How's this?" He pulled a sweater over his head.

"Perfect fit," said Ryan. "Just one question, squirt. How come you're not coming out to track anymore? Give up?"

Gavy exchanged glances with Ashley, looking for help. He shrugged.

"Joe says I'm too small," he said. "Told me to run around in the schoolyard and play tag. He said he wouldn't train anybody, like, for the Riders, until Grade Seven. So I'm getting ready."

"Is that right, Ms. Wellesley?" asked Kathryn, as the teacher approached.

"It's true," she said. "Joe was willing to take all of you for training. That's because he could work with you in the same way he works with me, the Riders, even the rest of his high school team."

"But why not Gavy?" asked Kathryn.

"Remember back in the fall, when we went out playing tag a few times?"

Along with the others, Matt nodded.

"You mean when Baz and Ryan wouldn't join us?" asked Kathryn.

"Thought it was too juvenile," said Ashley. "I thought that, too."

"That's when they did a fast run around Centrefield-Varcoe instead," said Matt, remembering.

"Fast? Yeah," said Baz. "We thought it was fast at the time. I ran the 3000 in only a minute more!"

Ms. Wellesley smiled. "Well, Joe has firm convictions. Hard training works — that's what you guys are doing, same as

Olympic athletes. But Joe won't train people unless they're in high school. And want to. And have some drive."

"Gavy wants to. And he sure has the drive."

"He's too short," said Ryan.

"I'll get over being short," said Gavin. "But you'll always be stupid. Joe says he'll coach me when I hit Grade Seven."

"Meanwhile," said Ashley, holding up another of the *Lovey Larks* sweaters. "What do we wear for track and field? We sure can't wear *these*."

"We'll think of something. It's only the end of March," said Ms. Wellesley. "We have two months."

Matt suddenly realized that high school wasn't that far off.

***

Matt had expected the visit to Queen's University with his mother and sister would be boring. He was not wrong.

Not ordinary boring, as in some classes. Not forever boring, like sitting in a doctor's waiting room. Not impatient boring, as in the time-that-lasts-forever-in-the-dressing-room-before-a-hockey-game boring.

No. This was boring as in: "I- am-being-dragged-by-the-neck-to-places-I-don't-want-to-go-boring." As in, "They-think-I-can't-look-after-myself." As in, "Who cares?"

Their guide, a girl not much older than Cathy-Marie, smiled politely. "This is a sample of a single residence room on a study floor," she said. They'd been put in a group of eight: three students, four parents, and Matt.

"We are on the sixth floor. This is Victoria Hall."

From the window, Matt peered down onto the street below. To the south, Lake Ontario glistened blue in the pale, March-morning sunshine.

"On each floor there is a common room, with a kitchen, a television; washrooms are single." The guide smiled at Matt as though she expected him to be interested.

"On a study floor like this," the guide continued, "the rules are: quiet at all times."

Matt could think of nothing more boring. Except maybe this tour.

"On other floors, there is a quiet hour after ten p.m."

"You mean nothing ever happens here?" Matt mumbled to himself, just at a time when the guide had stopped talking. Everyone heard him.

"Well, not nothing," said the guide. "A lot of studying goes on here."

"How boring," mumbled Matt. "My sister will love it."

The group shuffled into the hall, where they were met by a huge blue bear dressed in a plaid waistcoat and a tam.

"Bubba-bubba-bubba-bubba," said the bear, lifting his front paws to appear even larger.

"And this is Boo Hoo, the bear," said the guide.

"Yabba-dabba-doo," said the bear.

"He's Queens' mascot. He appears at sports games and other functions."

"Boo Hoo Boo Hoo, BOO! BOO! BOO!" said the bear.

The bear lumbered through the group, offering hugs to the girls and mothers. He shook hands with the two fathers in the group.

"He's named after the original Boo Hoo, who was a real bear cub adopted by students as a mascot in 1922. Four other Boo Hoos followed. The last real bear Boo Hoo was in 1952, then the University banned live pets."

Boo Hoo reared back as though in horror, then covered his face with his paws. Recovering, he moved toward Matt. He reached out for a hug, which Matt avoided. The bear then attempted a high-five. Matt tried to join in, but the bear missed his uplifted hand on purpose, and faked a stumble.

The bear swung around and draped one arm over Matt's shoulder.

"Don't ever be a bear," he said in Matt's ear. "It stinks in here."

Matt laughed, though not so loudly anyone might think he was not still bored.

The guide moved on down the hall with the students and parents following. The bear shuffled along with Matt at the end of the parade.

"They stick you with this tour, kid?" asked the bear.

"My sister," Matt replied.

"Oh, yeah, sisters," said the bear. "I've got two at home. But mine are younger than me."

"That might be better."

"Think of it this way," said the bear. "She comes here next year, you'll be rid of her. Most of the time, anyway."

Another group approached from the opposite direction.

"BOO! BOO! BOO! BOO! BOO! BOO! BOO! BOO!" said the bear, trying to be frightening. People in the new group smiled.

"I try to be scary, but it just don't work," the bear told Matt. "What's your sport? Let me guess. Chess, right?"

"Huh?"

"Your sport. You look like you've got to have a sport. That your sister?" the bear lifted a padded paw toward Cathy-Marie.

Matt nodded.

"She doesn't have a sport," said the bear. "I can tell."

"She studies," said Matt, as though it was a disease.

"She'll have lots of that to do here. But your sport?"

"Hockey. I mean, and track. Yeah. Hockey and track."

"Track? You run distance?"

"Fifteen hundred."

"Oh, great. A middle-distance star. You know what it's like to have a bear on your back. How would you like to have this bear on your back?"

The bear jumped on Matt's back and said, "Giddyup!"

Matt staggered a few steps down the hallway before the bear jumped off.

"Now you know what a real bear on your back is like!" said Boo Hoo.

The bear flapped a paw against an outer window. Down on the street, six runners were in motion: two in a group down by the lake, and four others moving in various directions.

"Heck, maybe you'll come to Queen's," said the bear. "You can get lots of training in here. There's a lot of runners around."

"We work out on the track twice a week," said Matt. "We go outdoors now if the weather is decent."

"What grade are you in?" asked the bear.

"Going into Grade Nine," said Matt.

"Four years. That's not long. So, yeah. Track. That's good. Wish I had taken track."

The bear slipped into the nearest stairwell. Just before he disappeared, he stuck his head back out and waved.

"Just don't be a bear," he said. "It's too hard to scare people."

13

Mud Happens

April is a cruel month. One day it's almost May and sunny and warm, and the next day the wind bites again like March. It is a confused month that can mix early flowers with rain and snow.

And mud.

"This sucks," said Baz.

Baz and Matt had started out on a run that Saturday morning from S.T. Lovey school. It was to be a slow, long run. Their route took them from the school down Courtice Road to Darlington Provincial Park.

Their aim had been to include some cross-country in their long, slow run. Joe had urged them to get out and run outdoors. So they had waited until the first warm, sunny day and headed out — and the park seemed like the perfect place. Several hiking trails criss-crossed the park. This would give them some up and downhill running to break up the monotony.

When they had started, it was a perfectly sunny morning. Twenty minutes later, when they entered the park, the rain started. Not the nice, gentle, soothing rain that runners like. No, this was a heavy, nasty, cold downpour; a rain that came from buckets, straight down, soaking the runners before they had time to seek shelter.

"*Really* sucks," Baz repeated.

"There's a pavilion around the corner," said Matt. "We'll duck in there until this lets up."

They continued around the bend and put their heads down for the slight uphill run to the pavilion. With their heads down from the rain and the mild climb, they weren't aware of the other runner until he came up behind them as they reached the shelter.

"Beautiful day for a little run," said the man.

Matt turned to see Tony Tuchuk step into the pavilion with them.

"Stone the crows!" said Tony. "It's Matt Thompson and Baz Amin!"

"Tony," he said. "What are you doing here?"

"I could ask the same question," said the school custodian. "But I won't. I can see you are running. Well, that's what I'm doing, too." He grinned, widely.

"I knew that," said Baz.

Matt looked up. That's when he saw the bicycles.

"Where'd all the bikes come from?" Baz asked.

About two dozen riders, complete with helmets, mountain bikes, and colourful gear, had also taken shelter under the open pavilion.

"Stone the crows, if ain't Tony!" said one of the cyclists, doing a poor job of imitating Tony's English accent.

Tony was dressed in racing shorts, a T-shirt from the Alfred Shrubb 3rd Annual 8-Kilometre Road Race, and a painter's cap which he now lifted to shake out the water, revealing thin wisps of hair that failed to cover the bald crown.

"Our race is going to be a little testy today," he said, more to Tony than to Matt and Baz.

"Race?" asked Matt.

"Yeah. This is our annual spring cross-country hill climb," said the cyclist. "All these guys came out to give it a try."

Matt peered out from under the roof of the pavilion into the pouring rain. One hiking trail disappeared into the overhanging trees.

"Three laps. Up the hill, around, back down, and up again. About a kilometre each lap."

"On bicycles?" said Baz, also looking up the bicycle path.

"On bicycles. Except for old Tony here."

Tony laughed. "Boys, this is Mel Hawes. He's the race direc-tor for the annual Darlington Hill-and-Dale. It's the world's only bike race in which a runner is allowed to enter," he said.

"Race the bikes?"

"Oh, yes, goodness, this uphill portion is tough enough that I can actually run faster uphill than these guys can bike. Of course, they pick that up on the way down."

"You race against the bikes?" Matt still couldn't believe it.

"Don't they, like, run over you or anything?" asked Baz.

"Oh, I keep out of the way."

Several of the cyclists at the far end of the pavilion called out.

"Hey, Mel! We about ready to start? It's too cold to stand here shivering."

Matt noticed he was also feeling the cold; his muscles quiv-ered. Baz was doing the same.

"Don't want to stand around after you've warmed up," said Tony. "Best to get started."

Matt couldn't believe it. "You're going to run in this?" he asked.

"In what?" asked Tony.

"In the rain! It's pouring!"

"So? You're made of sugar? You're going to melt in the rain?" asked Tony. "Hey, you guys want to join me in this race?

Three runners against eighteen bicycles."

Matt looked at Baz. Baz looked back. As though on a signal, the downpour started to let up. A slight drizzle continued.

"I could use the company," said Tony.

"We couldn't be any wetter," said Baz.

Matt shrugged. "Why not?"

***

The start was simple. Mel Hawes said, "Go." Then he clicked his stopwatch.

Matt and Baz lunged ahead, with Tony Tuchuk following, and eighteen bicycles rolling behind them.

The dirt path, wide at first, narrowed as it steepened. The runners broke faster from the start than the bicycles. They reached the foot of the uphill path through the woods first. On the narrow uphill path, bicycles had no room to pass. But there was little danger of that. The trail was so steep, even the runners struggled upward at a walking pace. They clambered up the steep slope, grabbing bushes and branches for handholds.

"I can see why you beat the bicycles," said Baz.

"Yeah, I'd hate to carry a bicycle up this slope," said Matt.

"It's different," said Tony.

Twice during the first climb, Tony had taken the lead. When that happened, Matt and Baz pushed forward, leapfrogging ahead.

"Two laps to go," said Tony.

At the top, the woods opened onto a grass-covered playing field. The trail skirted along the edge of the woods for 100 metres or so. Running on the level ground seemed effortless now.

But half a minute later, they plunged back into the wooded area. The trail dropped before them, even steeper going down than it had been going up.

"Watch the branches!" said Tony, pushing by both boys and almost dropping out of sight into the bramble. "Watch my steps!"

The two boys plunged after him, using their heels as brakes. Matt soon learned to use short, quick steps, as Tony was doing.

"Woowee!" shouted Baz from behind as he leapt over a tiny brook.

They broke into the open and continued downhill. The field levelled off again. The pavilion was off to their left. They followed Tony, spread out now behind the custodian.

"Five thirty!" yelled a man holding a stopwatch.

"Two more!" yelled Tony from ten metres ahead.

"I can see why the bikes are slower on that trail!" grunted Baz.

"Save your breath," Matt replied.

The wet, dirty trail had now turned to grease. Matt slipped and caught himself with a free arm. Ahead, Tony powered forward, his shoes finding traction in the grime.

"Coming through!" Tony yelled.

Matt looked up. The top of the trail was still thirty metres ahead. Two cyclists struggled up the last portion of the path, bicycles slung over one shoulder.

Tony passed the first, then the second. Seconds later, Matt skirted off the trail to move around both cyclists. He could hear Baz behind him.

"Gangway!" yelled Tony.

Matt followed Tony onto the downhill trail. Just before he made that plunge, he glanced back to see the two cyclists reach the top, mount their bikes, and head after them.

"They'll catch us," he said, to no one in particular.

"Branch!" Matt yelled, holding back the limb of a sapling for Baz to duck under.

Two cyclists bounced into the air ahead, their bikes nose-first down the slope. Like airsick eagles, Matt thought.

Halfway down, the two cyclists they had passed going up passed the runners, handbrakes squealing, tires bouncing, riders laughing like maniacs in the wet and the mud.

"Eleven minutes!" yelled the timekeeper as they started the third lap.

This time on the upward climb they passed six bikes in all. A portion of the uphill trail was so steep it forced the cyclists to hoist their bikes onto one shoulder and walk — not easy to do through the bramble and shrubs on greasy, muddy footing.

"The rain is our friend," Tony said at the top.

The three runners, the cyclists, the bikes, most of the trees, and the trail were by now pure mud. Mud coloured their shirts, clogged their shoes, and covered their hair, hands, and elbows.

Matt slipped twice on the uphill greasy mud, falling *splat*! Face-first.

Climbing on the third and final lap, Matt and Baz no longer ran. They clambered, sometimes on all fours, slipping on the soupy trail. Tony had long since zoomed ahead, finding traction where the boys could find only grease.

The final downhill was more a slippery slide than a run. Matt and Baz balanced their way over knolls, knocked their heads on branches, and surfed down the greasy churnings left by the bicycles.

"Seventeen forty!" yelled the timekeeper as Matt and Baz crossed the finish together.

A mud-covered Tony greeted them at the finish line with an old-fashioned handshake.

"Was that the workout you had planned for today?" Tony

asked with a grin — his almost-white teeth now being the only part of him not caked in mud.

"I thought cross-country was bad," said Baz.

"It's only mud," said Tony. "Besides, isn't it worth it to say you beat eighteen bicycles in a race?"

"Wouldn't miss it!" said Baz.

"Me neither," said Matt.

"So you thought about the Vikings yet?" asked Tony. The question came out of nowhere.

"Vikings?" asked Baz.

"Yeah, Clarington Vikings. Track club," said Tony.

"We're training with the Riders," said Baz.

"Yeah," said Matt.

"That's just for the spring," said Tony. "Wasn't that the deal? Joe traded you some coaching so that Ms. Wellesley would get back to training with Joe?"

"Something like that," said Matt.

"So what about after that? Come June, Joe's going to cut you loose. You need a club to run with over the summer or you'll lose your conditioning."

"We're hoping Joe would … invite us to join," began Baz. "As full members. That's what we hope. We…"

"Get your 1500-metre time to four thirty and he will," said Tony.

"You think he would?" asked Baz.

"Yes," Tony replied. "He's not going to budge on inviting you to join the Riders without some really good performances. Maybe not even then."

Matt scuffed the toe of his shoe on the ground. He wasn't sure anymore if he really did want to join the Riders.

"We'll show him," he said, though he knew he didn't really mean it.

"Even if you do, he'll likely want you to change schools, too," said Tony.

"How do you know that?" asked Matt.

"That's the way he works. Feels it better if the athletes in his club are with him all the time. Good for the school, too. He's a good coach. One of the best in Canada."

Baz was silent for a minute.

"But we'd have to get a ride to school each day," he said. "Or take a bus. Forty minutes on the bus."

"I guess my mom could take us," said Matt without enthusiasm. "But I haven't asked her yet."

"Don't start planning the omelette before the eggs have been laid," said Tony. "You run some times to impress Joe, then you can worry about the details," said Tony. "But I'd gather all the options. Have you looked at what coaching they have at Courtice Secondary?"

Matt shrugged.

"And the Vikings have a weird distance and cross-country coach," said Tony.

Matt and Baz shrugged in unison. The rain had started again and the mud was now soaking into their clothes.

"Who?" asked Baz.

Tony grinned.

"That would be me," said Tony. He looked down at his T-shirt. "Oh, dear," he said. "I've got my T-shirt dirty." He brushed away at some of the wet mud.

Baz laughed. "Just what is the Alfie Shr ... that shirt you're wearing?"

"That's from the Alfie Shrubb run in Bowmanville," said Tony. "Coming up again in June. You guys should try it."

"A marathon?" asked Matt.

"Never, never," said Tony. "Eight kilometres. Alfie Shrubb

was an English runner. One hundred years ago, he set records all over the place. Moved to Bowmanville after his racing days were over. Every year now, the Bowmanville Museum puts on this road race for him. Maybe you should try it this year. Anyway, you guys should head home before you seize up. You going my way?"

"You're not going to wait for the bikes?" asked Baz.

"They'll know they've been beaten," said Tony. "It's happened before."

14

Decisions, Decisions

The very next day, Matt received a phone call. *The* phone call.

"Who is it?" he mouthed to his mother as she held the phone out toward him. *She could have put it on hold*, he thought.

His mother just shrugged. She really didn't know.

"Matt?"

The voice at the other end of the phone sounded far away. Mild static scrambled the line.

"Hello?" said Matt, not sure who he was talking to.

"Sorry, I don't seem to have a good connection. I'm on a cell phone."

"Hello?" Matt repeated. He could barely make out the voice. "Hello?"

"Matt, I'm … at the track yesterday and…" The voice kept fading in and out, the crackling mudding up the message at key places. Matt still couldn't make out the owner of the voice.

"Hello? Hello?" Matt repeated, not sure of how to deal with the problem.

"These darned things," said the voice, clearly now Joe Calder's voice. "Can you…" The voice faded one more time, then came back. "Okay?"

"You're fading out," Matt said. "I can't hear you."

" ...*crackle* get to the top of the hill ... *crackle* ... call you back."

The line went dead.

Matt hung up and waited.

Three minutes later, the phone rang again.

"Hello," Matt said, in a stunning feat of originality.

"Hello, Matt. Can you hear me now?"

This time the connection was perfectly clear and the voice was perfectly Joe's. Matt said so.

"That's great, that's great. Matt, I called you at home because I wanted to talk to you without the others around. Matt, I've been very impressed with your progress these past few weeks. To tell the truth, I really didn't think any of your group had a chance."

"Thanks ... I think."

"Let me put it up front, Matt. Would you be interested in joining the Riders? As a full member?"

"I would..."

"Of course you don't have to answer right away. You can call me next Tuesday and let me know. And promise you won't mention this to any of the other runners."

"I'm sorry, what was that?"

"The last thing I want over the next four weeks is to have others hounding me to join as well. Or having to explain. So you'll promise me that? Whatever you decide?"

"I promise," Matt replied.

"Okay, so here's the deal. I'm offering you a chance to join the Riders. That way, I can train you all the way through high school. That's the other part. In order to join the Riders, you'll have to transfer to Dwyer High School. That way you can also run for the Dwyer school track team, which I also coach. It's easier that way."

"Gee, thanks, Joe, I..."

"No problem. Now, with the club thing there are some costs involved. I'll talk to your parents about that when you've made your decision. Call me Tuesday. Here. At this number. You got call display? Then you've got my cellphone number. I'll try not to be out of range."

"Okay."

"And just to repeat: please don't mention this to the others. As I said, I'd have waited until after the district track meet, but school registration deadline is a week from Friday. You'll have to make your decision and apply by then. So time is important."

The line went quiet for several seconds.

"Matt?"

A pause. Matt searched for words. Joe continued.

"I take on only two or three new runners each year. Most of my runners end up on track scholarships at universities. Train with me and you will have a solid running career."

"Thanks, Joe. I won't tell."

"Good. And call me next Tuesday. See you at the track."

The line went dead.

***

"When do you have to know?" Mrs. Thompson asked.

Cathy-Marie stood with three university envelopes in her hands. Her mother looked sympathetic.

"June 15," said Cathy-Marie. "But I already know."

"You've made a decision already?" asked her father.

"Western, U of T, Queen's," said Cathy-Marie. "What's to decide?"

"Must be easy," said Matt.

"Hmph!" replied his sister. "As if you had big decisions to make. Just you wait. Some day…"

Matt thought that at times like this his sister sounded more like a parent than his mother or father.

"Matt has decisions, too," said his father. "Don't you Matt?"

"What? Will that be Courtice or Courtice," replied Cathy-Marie. "Big deal."

Mr. Thompson cleared his throat. "It's more than that. He has to pick between Courtice Secondary School and a high school in Oshawa. Between the Durham Riders and the Clarington Vikings."

Mrs. Thompson pursed her lower lip. She recited: *"'I'm just as big for me,' said he, 'As you are big for you.'"*

"What's that supposed to mean?" said Cathy-Marie scornfully.

"It's a poem my father used to recite," said Mrs. Thompson. "He memorized it in the first grade. Let's see if I remember it."

She screwed up her right cheek and squinted. This helped her memory, for she began to recite:

"I met a little Elfman once,
Down where the lilies blow.
I asked him why he was so small,
And why he didn't grow.
He slightly frowned, and with his eye
He looked me through and through.
'I'm just as big for me,' said he,
'As you are big for you.'"

Cathy-Marie stood with her mouth open. "You *remember* that?" she said.

"Thanks, Mom," said Matt, embarrassed. "Thanks a lot."

"I remember because I Googled it just yesterday. It was written by John Kendrick Bangs about ninety years ago."

"They had the Internet *then*?" asked Matt. "Ninety years ago?"

"Some children!" replied Cathy-Marie.

"Enough of that," said Matt's father. "Your mother's trying to say that Matt's decision is just as big for him as your decision about university is for you."

"Just as your decision is as important for you as your father's decision about moving back to London. And about my clients. And…

"We're moving back to *London*?" said Cathy-Marie.

"I didn't say we were moving," replied her mother. "I said your father has had a job offer. With his old company. Back in London."

"But I…" said Matt.

"Cool-o," said Cathy-Marie, scornfully.

"Cool-o?" Matt replied. "Did you say Cool-o? Nobody says Cool-o. It's the uncoolest thing anybody could say!"

"Child!"

"Fat lot moving means to you," retorted Matt. "You haven't even made a friend here. But for me…"

"I did too!" said Cathy-Marie.

"Didn't!"

"Did!"

"Didn't!"

"Sounds like a logical argument to me," said Mr. Thompson. "Now why don't we all go sit in a corner and suck our thumbs for a while?"

Matt shrugged.

Cathy-Marie stormed from the room, stomped up the stairs, stamped into her room and slammed the door behind her. A picture fell off the wall in the hallway.

"And all she has to do is decide where to spend our money," said Mr. Thompson. "It must be nice. What would she do if she had a *real* decision, like the rest of us."

Matt knew it was strange that he understood what his father was saying.

***

Much later the same afternoon, Cathy-Marie came slinking out of her room. Quietly, she sought out Matt, who sat mindlessly, angrily, in front of the computer playing his favourite game.

"I'm sorry."

That's all she said. Matt pushed buttons on the joystick, jammed the stick forward, and fired repeatedly. The creature on the screen would not die.

"I said I was sorry."

On the screen, the multi-headed green monster turned into a small kitten and Matt entered a level of the game he had never seen before.

"I dissed you bad, and I shouldn't have. It was … immature and juvenile of me."

Matt looked at his sister. She had been crying.

"It's okay," he said. "It's no big deal."

Cathy-Marie lifted her eyes from the floor and smiled. "But it is a big deal. You have to choose between starting high school with your friends or starting at a strange school. That's a big deal. Grade Nine is a big deal. I remember my first day in Grade Nine. The school was huge, the rooms were huge, the classes were huge, the other students were, I mean, huge, like, grown up almost. I felt so small."

"It won't be like that."

His sister smiled. "It *will* be like that. I went from being a really important person in Grade Eight, where every teacher and almost all the kids knew my name. Then there I was in a new school without any of my friends in any of my classes. There were sixty students in my Grade Eight class. Forty of us went to the same high school. You'd think we'd all be buddies, right? Wrong. Would you believe that in a high school of 1200 students I would sometimes go all day long and never see anybody I knew?"

"Wouldn't be like that. I'd be on the track team."

"You mean at Dwyer? You're going to be a big jock, right? Well, maybe if every day you're training with the track club, you'd make some friends. But they'd mostly be seniors. They won't pay a lot of attention to Grade Niners. Not at first. Believe me."

"There'd be Kevin, and Baz, and, Mark, and Noah, and ..."

"Baz's your buddy, right?"

"Well, kind of. On the track, anyway. We make each other better."

Cathy-Marie smiled. "You talk as though you've already made up your mind. Are you sure Baz has been given the same offer you have?"

"What do you mean?"

"I mean, has this Joe guy invited Baz to run with the Riders? Didn't you say he asked you to promise not to tell the others?"

"Yeah, I guess I just assumed he meant the girls. And Robert."

"And you can't ask without breaking your promise."

"Yeah. I never thought of Baz," Matt shifted in his chair, which had a broken spring. "I mean, I just assumed he'd be invited, too. Now I don't know what to think. Riders, Vikings. Courtice, Dwyer. To tell you the truth, I can't make up my mind."

"I'm the same with the universities," said his sister. "They all look good. But I have trouble imagining how I would do there. It makes me grouchy."

"So I've noticed."

"So what about Courtice? Would you be on the track team if you went there? And what about the Riders?"

Matt swivelled from side to side in his seat. "That's the tough part. I can be in the Riders only if I go to Dwyer. That's Joe's rules. "If I go to Courtice, I could be on the track team, but there's not much coaching. I'd have to join the Clarington Vikings. That's about the only other club. Or maybe the Oshawa Legion."

"But...?"

"Ashley will be going to Courtice. If I went to Dwyer I wouldn't see her much at all."

"Oh, I see!" replied Cathy-Marie, in that knowing voice that adults use when young people talk about girlfriends or boyfriends. "That's important, I take it."

"Ashley's why I wanted to join the Riders. To impress her. Then when she found out I *might* join the Riders she almost bit my head off."

"You don't mean that literally."

"Huh?"

"You mean that *figuratively*. That's your big word for the day, Matthew. Figuratively. Still, it is a very violent image."

"Sometimes I wonder about you, sis."

"Sorry. I get carried away. You were saying?"

"I wouldn't mind joining the Vikings. The coach is interesting. He's the custodian at my school."

"You mean that old, thin guy who was at the race last fall? The one at, where was it, Ganaraska?"

"Last month he and Baz and I raced a whole bunch of bicycles on a cross-country race. We beat them all. All of them. But that Tony, that old dude was so far out front of us that he could have gone for a walk before we finished. In fact, he did. That dude can run! And he's so old!"

"And he coaches the Vikings?"

"Yup."

"Seems like that would be kind of fun."

Matt thought for a moment. He pressed the reset button to start the video game again.

"I dunno," he said. "Some of Joe's runners have run for Canada. Two went in the World Cross-Country Championships in Ireland a few years ago. Others have gone on to get big scholarships."

"It sounds like serious track."

"And Ms. Wellesley, our teacher. She's training under Joe. Maybe to make it to the Olympics."

"That's serious."

"Yeah."

"So it sounds like you have to decide between serious and fun."

"Huh?"

"Whether you want to be a serious runner with Joe, or to enjoy running with the Vikings. Isn't that it?"

"Well, maybe."

Cathy-Marie rose.

"And you could run for fun now, in high school, and get serious two or three years from now. Ever hear of burnout? That could happen, you know. Anyway, I'm sorry I got mad and insulted you. It wasn't fair. We should be mature and be nice to each other. Remember what our grandfather used to say about stuff? He'd say, 'Your brain will figure it out, your brain will figure it out.'"

"Like riding a bike."

"Did he do that with you, too? Dad would get sick of holding me up. But Granddad would hold onto the seat and balance me. I think I was only four. And he would just say, 'Your brain will figure it out.' And it did. One day I just pedalled away from him. I thought of that when I was up in my room this afternoon. That with this decision about university, I'm going to let my brain figure it out. You should do that same."

"Then I don't have to do anything?"

"Your brain can't figure it out alone. That's another thing Granddad said. You have to feed your brain the stuff it needs to decide. You shovel in the facts. *Then* your brain can figure it out."

Matt glanced back at the video game. His character was in a room with a stairway to the left, an open window on the right, and spiders on the walls.

"So we don't have to worry about it, right?"

"Just get the facts right. That's what I'm doing. Trust that when the times comes, we'll know what's right."

Matt pressed a few buttons. "I have three days to decide," he said. "But I can't tell anyone until after the district meet," said Matt.

"What does that have to do with price of orange juice?"

"Joe's rules. And I kind of had to promise," said Matt. "The meet should be interesting. Baz, me, Ryan. We've been training all year."

"The three of you?"

"Yeah. Ryan came in third in the school race, so I guess he's going to run at the district meet, too."

"Why wouldn't he?"

"He's the guy who cut his leg last fall kicking in the glass door, remember? So at our little track meet on the school grounds, Baz and me, we burned everybody. Then Ryan, he sort of, like, jogged through it and still came in third. Coach doesn't want him to race hard until his leg is ready. So Baz and me, we just ran away from everybody. Funny, though, trying to run the

1500-metre dodging trees after training on the track."

"And you won?"

"The teacher, Ms. Wellesley, says Ryan's getting close."

"Isn't Ryan that guy with the spiked red hair and all the rings? He's the coolest kid ever. Where's the race?"

"The district finals? At the Civic Stadium."

"You're going to run on that indoor track at this time of year? In June?" she said.

"The Stadium is outdoors," Matt replied. "A 400-metre track. It's great."

Cathy-Marie looked at Matt for a moment. "I hope you do well," she said. "I really mean that."

"Cool," Matt replied. Then he looked up at his sister.

"I mean, cool-o," he added.

Cathy-Marie smiled back.

15

Track Meet

The night before the Clarington Regional School Track Meet, it rained and rained and rained and rained.

But the day of the meet dawned with clear skies and bright, early June sunshine. When the athletes from S. T. Lovey Public School stepped off the bus at the Oshawa Civic Stadium, the day could only be described as perfect.

The sun shone. The sky was blue. Birds sang sweetly.

Ashley smiled at Matt in a way that gave him shivers.

However, the rain had left the infield soggy and muddy. The runners quickly found that just walking across the infield turned the turf into greasy, slippery, ugly mud.

Water stood ankle-deep in the lower field behind the stadium.

"Stay in the stands," said Ms .Wellesley. "Don't get your shoes and socks wet and muddy. Stay clean. Don't eat hot dogs until after your events."

"Aww…" said Gavy.

"You'll be sorry if you don't," said the teacher. "Make sure you don't eat anything for two hours before your event."

"I thought that was an hour," said Ashley. "And I thought it was swimming. You know, giving you, like, cramps and stuff."

"That's the same idea," said Ms. Wellesley. "Digesting food

takes energy. Save your strength for your event."

"What about Ryan?" asked Baz. "Is he going to be able to run?"

Ms. Wellesley smiled. "The short answer is yes. Now all we have to do is convince Ryan. I think he's ready. Joe thinks he's ready. I talked to the rules committee, and they've agreed to let him run. Schools are allowed to enter a third person if the committee is satisfied that the performance is possible."

"Which means, like, what?" asked Ashley.

"Which means his training times show he'd be competitive," said Ms. Wellesley. "So you've got all day to work on him. If he believes he'll do well, he'll do well."

Matt and Baz exchanged glances.

"All day? When is the senior 1500 metre?"

"Second last event. Right after the girls' 1500 — so Kathryn, Ashley, you should get ready for that. The last event is the 3000. Anybody who wants to can run that."

"So what, two o'clock?"

"About then," said the teacher. "Until then, relax. Eat early. Watch the events. Stay off the infield, you'll get your shoes muddy."

It's good to have Ms. Wellesley acting like a coach again, Matt thought.

***

Nobody could mistake Ryan, with his orange hair and nose-and-ear rings.

"You running?" asked Baz, as Ryan joined them at the far end of the track. They were waiting for the 1500-metre race to start.

"Tha's right, bro," answered Ryan.

About fifteen athletes from several schools jiggled and bounced and fidgeted. The 1500 started directly across the track from the finish line in front of the grandstand. On the 400-metre track, the race would be four laps — minus the top curve. The runners waited in the extra alcove of the back straight.

"You running in that?" asked Baz, pointing at Ryan's shirt.

The uniforms the school council had bought for the team had been too small. Matt remembered the day they tried them on. The tops would only fit Gavy, or others from fifth grade down. The senior class had told the principal. Matt thought the outfits had been sent back.

"Right as grass," said Ryan.

Ryan had taken one of the A-tops. To make it fit, he had cut extra room under the arms, cut the shoulder straps, and lengthened them with extra cloth. He had pulled the result over his head. It came down to the bottom of his rib cage. Across his chest was written: *Lovey Larks*.

"The principal sees you, she's gonna gash your other leg."

"Be worth it," said Ryan with a grin. "You two not gonna wear school colours for this race? This is our last chance to run for Lovey, you know."

"We'll let our speed get people's attention," said Baz.

The other runners were dressed in a variety of gear. Some wore knee-length shorts, T-shirts below crotch level, and long, floppy laces.

"Half these guys gonna trip on their ties," said Ryan, hitching his jerry-rigged shirt and knee-length nylon shorts.

Early in training with Ms. Wellesley, they had learned that sloppy, cool laces and clothes didn't work on the track. A shoelace that came untied in a race was definitely uncool.

While they waited at the southeast corner of the track, they half watched the girls' 1500-metre race taking place on the track in front of them. The lead runners from that race ran by. Kathryn, her face twisted in effort, held third place. Seconds later Ashley came by, in next-to-last place.

"Go get 'em, Ashes!" said Matt.

Ashley gave him a strange look that Matt could not interpret.

A minute or so later, the bell lap rang from across the finish line. Matt turned his attention in that direction. Kathryn, now in fourth position in the main pack, was falling back. As she came around the top turn, they could see others pass her.

"Kathryn's not doing well today," said Baz. "That's not like her."

"Yeah, but watch Ashley," said Ryan, pointing.

Right then, Ashley began a move; they could see the space increase between her and the last runner.

"Looks like she's going to start a charge," said Baz.

Ashes swung wide on the turn, passing one, two, three runners. As she passed, Matt, Baz, and Ryan jumped and yelled and cheered. Before their eyes she passed two more runners. By the time she started down the back straight, she had caught the tail end of the main pack of runners. On the straight she kept a full lane to the outside.

"What's she doing?" asked Ryan.

"She's in the passing lane," said Baz.

"And look at her go," said Matt.

When the lead runners hit the end of the back straight with 200 metres to go, the main pack began to string out. Ashley continued on the outside, passing more runners. At the bottom curve, the boys watched as she passed Kathryn, moving into fourth place. Third. Coming off the curve, she eased into second place.

"Man, she's moving!" said Ryan.

"She's gonna die!" said Baz, disappointed. "She started too early!"

The race now came down to a sprint for the finish. Ashley rose high and held her poise. Her main opponent, in first place, tried to respond, but began to tie up halfway up the straight-away.

Ashes didn't die. Instead, she sped by, looking loose and easy in her run.

She won by several metres.

"Did you see that!" said Baz, not as a question.

"What a race!" said Matt. "She pulled all of that out on the last lap! From second last to first!"

The Lovey students in the stands yelled and stamped for Ashley in her victory.

"Get ready for your start," said the race official. An older man with a trimmed beard wearing a golf shirt from the Ontario Games strode over to the start line.

"As soon as they get the track cleared, we're ready to go."

Matt shuffled into line with the others, jiggling nervously from foot to foot.

16

Bell Lap

F ifteen-hundred metres, boys," called the race official in overly dramatic tones only a teacher trying to herd students could muster. "Senior boys."

"Them's us," said Ryan, holding out one leg and wiggling it sideways.

"Start in three minutes," said the official. "Be ready. Line up now."

Baz, Matt, and Ryan quickly fell into place along the start line. Others filled in to their right; then many in a row behind.

Matt wondered how many of the other runners had trained with track clubs. Those runners would be okay, he thought. But others not used to racing might cause start problems. Joe had warned them to beware of pushing.

The official waved to another race official at the start line.

"Okay, guys, be getting ready," said the official. He paused for a moment.

"Mark!" He raised one hand directly overhead.

Matt and ten other runners on the front line leaned forward on their toes. Matt cocked his left arm back, waiting for the signal. One runner to his left had dropped to a sprinter's starting crouch.

In the moment before the start of a race, Matt had noticed,

time seemed to stand still. Tensed for the starting signal, Matt was aware of small details: a buzzing fly that would not leave; a shout from a further field behind the stadium; a car rushing by on Thornton Road.

Bang! The starter's pistol gave off a puff of smoke. The starter dropped his arm at the same time.

Matt sprang forward. Ryan and Baz were at his side. To his right, three or four runners sprinted forward, bunching to the inside, moving toward Matt and his friends.

"Unfriendly fire at three o'clock," said Ryan.

Behind them, Matt could hear scrambling on the track. Someone pushed him once in the middle of the back. He almost lost his balance, stumbled forward, then regained his stride.

Several runners now filled the track ahead of them. Matt and Baz exchanged glances. Ryan swung wide to the right, to the outside of the track.

Running outside, Ryan would have to run further. Matt wondered about this. When the second runner bumped him and almost put him down, he realized what Ryan was doing.

Deftly, he moved beside Baz.

"Follow Ryan," he said.

Together, they moved two lanes to the outside. This allowed several runners to pant by them. But by the top of the first curve, they had all settled in. Those with too much ambition had sped ahead, and already the race pattern began to develop.

Coming off the first curve, Matt followed Baz. They moved back to the inside lane now, about six runners back of the leader. Ryan followed, dropping in behind Matt.

"Three laps! Three laps to go!" said the lap counter at the start line. A cheer began to rise from the grandstands.

As they came off the second curve, completing one lap, the starter held out his stop watch and counted out the time.

"Seventy-five … seventy-seven … seventy-nine … eighty-one…"

"Eighty for the first lap," said Baz, hardly even breathing hard. "That's about right."

"Umph," grunted Ryan from behind.

"Leader's at seventy-five," said Matt. "He's moving."

"He'll come back," said Baz.

The leader was a runner from Hobbs Senior. He wore long shorts, a baggy T-shirt, and a baseball cap.

"Yeah," said Ryan, whose breath already came in grunts.

"I hope," said Baz, as the leader started around the far curve.

On the second back straight they eased their way around two, then three runners. By the time they came out of the curve into the grandstand straight, Baz, Matt, and Ryan ran four-five-six — in that order.

"Two! Two laps to go!" said an official.

They passed the start line again.

"Two forty-two, two forty-three, two forty-four," the starter counted in a sing-song voice.

Matt tried to do the mental arithmetic, but couldn't. He knew that was not good. He would have to rely on the others for pacing. With two laps to go, the easy part of the race had disappeared. Now the work began.

Down the back straight for the third time, they passed one more runner: three-four-five. On the top curve, Baz moved around still another.

The runner from Hobbs powered on. His stride, which had looked awkward, did not let up. He held his position ten full metres ahead of Baz, with Matt and Ryan following.

The crowd in the stands had come alive. A wall of noise and cheers welled up. The announcer's voice blared over the speakers:

"On the track now, the seniors boys' 1500 metres. Going into the bell lap, it's Serge Deanike leading the field, followed by Baz Amin, Matt Thompson, and Ryan Abolins, all of S.T. Lovey."

The voice echoed as they poured down the straight. Baz had now begun his move, closing the gap on the Hobbs runner with each step.

Ding-a-ding-a-ding-a-ding!

Bell lap: last lap — a signal that no runner could mistake.

Baz moved around Deanike at the bell, smoothly moving into the lead as they started around the top curve. Matt followed. Behind, Ryan breathed in grunting gasps, heavy feet slapping on the pavement.

But just as he caught the Hobbs runner, Matt watched in dismay as his competitor surged away: 1 metre, 2 metres, until he parked on Baz's back 6 metres ahead. Coming out of the top of the curve, Matt heard a grunt, and suddenly Ryan was at his elbow, orange hair glowing in the sunshine, rings bobbling, twinkling.

Ryan, too, went by him, gaining 1, 2 metres before sliding into the lane in front of him.

All Matt could now see going down the back straight was Ryan's silly top. Somewhere ahead were Baz and the runner from Hobbs. His lungs began to burn, his legs hurt, his body calling out for oxygen. Time slowed. He felt as though he was running in thick syrup. What did Granddad say? Molasses in January?

Coming down the back straight, Matt saw that the Hobbs runner had retaken the lead. Baz began to fall back, struggling.

And it was Ryan closing the gap.

The roar from the stands pulled Matt back into the race. At trackside he saw his sister and parents standing just beyond the 200-metre mark, arms waving in circles. And Ms. Wellesley, too, yelling words he couldn't hear, cheering on her students. And, for a reason he could not understand, there was Tony, standing by a mud puddle, both hands squeezing mud balls, yelling more words Matt could not hear.

Suddenly, with gobs of soupy mud in each hand, Tony started slapping his cheeks.

The sight jarred him.

Matt rose on his toes. Half a lap, 200 metres.

He came into the final curve, knees high, arms pumping. He caught Baz at the top of the bend. They came into the final straight one-two-three: Serge Deanike, Ryan, and Matt.

Matt swung wide a full lane and lifted his knees even higher and kicked. Hard.

His steps came now in slow motion. Ryan's back came closer, Serge in his baggy T-shirt, too. The crowd noise became a wall, with grimacing, shouting faces, mouths opened, fixed in his mind.

The finish-line judges, stopwatches in their hands, leaned forward with frozen faces; a struggling runner on the track almost lapped by the leaders, half turned, like a photograph, checking over his shoulder.

"Four fifty-eight, four fifty-nine, five minutes…"

Matt lunged for the line, catching Ryan, then Serge. But by then, they were over the line and cruising slowly to a halt.

Matt's breath came in gasps. He sucked air but couldn't get enough. He was aware of someone chasing him. First he thought it was Ryan, but no, someone chased Ryan, too, with his orange hair, and Baz, yes, Baz was there. And Serge had fallen to the track in exhaustion, until someone helped him up.

A hand grabbed Matt's arm, lifted it overhead.

"First place," said the race official. "First place."

Matt looked around to see who had won. The race official

who had grabbed him, still holding his arm aloft, repeated: "First place."

"Second!" said another, the official holding Ryan.

"Third!" came another, from Serge's crumpled form on the track.

Baz leaned over, hands on his knees, his breath in sucking sobs.

"Fourth," he said, "fourth." But no one held his hand aloft.

17

Ashley's Surprise

Baz slapped him on the back. "You're the champ, Matt!" The Hobbs runner came over and shook his hand.

"Great run," he said, still breathing hard.

"Thanks," Matt mumbled.

Ashley pushed up to the edge of the crowd. "Great run, Matt!" she yelled.

"You did great, too," Matt replied. The smile she flashed gave Matt goosebumps.

Ryan jogged over and draped one arm around Matt's shoulder. "I didn't even see you coming," said Ryan. "Out of the sun, like the fighter pilots of old: Matt Thompson guns down the opposition."

"Yeah, but it was this guy..." Matt pointed to the runner from Hobbs, "who set the pace. Great run, man," he said, and Serge nodded.

"Hey, next year we'll be teammates," said Serge.

"What do you mean?" asked Baz.

"Well, you guys are all from Lovey, right? So next year we could gang up to run for Courtice Secondary."

Baz and Matt exchanged glances. But it was Ryan who answered.

"Maybe, maybe not," Ryan said. "I'm going to be running for Dwyer."

Joe Calder appeared out of nowhere, tall, cool, and serene.

"Well done, guys," he said. To Baz he said, "Too bad. I thought you had this in the bag until your wheels fell off."

"That's all there was," said Baz, showing his usual smile despite his disappointment.

"Good kick, kid," Joe said to Matt. "You really lit your fire in that last half lap. Are you sure you don't want to change your mind?"

"About the Riders?" Matt replied. "No, I don't think so. It's too late anyway, isn't it?"

"Actually, yes," said Joe. "But I thought I'd ask. That was a great run. We'll get you into the Riders yet."

"What do you mean?" asked Ashley. She looked from Matt to Joe and back again. "You mean Matt isn't joining the Riders?"

"Naw," said Baz. "Matt and I decided we'd stick with the Clarington Vikings. Stick with our friends."

"Thanks, buddy," said Ryan.

"But I thought …" said Ashley, for once at a loss for words. "I mean, Joe called me, and said I was improving *really* well …"

Matt looked at Ashley, who returned a curious look. Only a few months earlier, he had dreamed of joining the Riders just to impress her.

"You mean Joe asked you to be a Rider, too?" asked Baz.

"You've got to be kidding!" said Kathryn. "Joe asked you to join the Riders?" Her look of disbelief showed on her face. "I mean." Her voice quivered slightly.

"But you were the one who was ticked when you thought I was joining the Riders!" said Matt. He tried not to swallow the hurt in his throat. "Baz and I are joining the Clarington Vikings. You said …" He faltered, then continued.

"Anyway, we can have a lot of fun that way." He motioned to Tony who had approached the edge of the group. "With this crazy coach." He paused. Ashley looked at him now and didn't blink.

"…I think," he added.

"We won't be teammates anymore," said Kathryn. "We won't run together."

"For goodness sake," said Tony. "Nobody's moving to the moon. You guys can still train together. You'll all be at the Dome next winter."

"That's right, I guess," said Kathryn.

Mud still covered Tony's hands and cheeks, but couldn't hide the grin on his face.

"Kind of thought you could use some limbering up," he said to Matt. "I'd shake hands but I'll get you all muddy, too."

Matt reached out and shook the custodian's hand anyway.

"Mud happens," he said. "It don't hurt."

Tony grinned and reached out to grasp Matt by the hand. "The coach of the Vikings will be pleased to have you," he said, and then turned and shook hands with Baz. "You, too?"

Baz smiled. "Me, too," he said. "Yeah, me, too. That way we can all still go to Courtice together next year."

"Ashley's been improving all spring," said Joe. "Don't make her feel bad about this. Maybe I should have been more open about this. But the deadlines…" He let his voice trail off. "You guys surprised me. All of you."

Matt looked at Ashley.

"A Durham Rider," he said. "Congratulations." For a moment, Matt found it hard to swallow. "Joe doesn't ask many runners to join."

Ashley looked down and blushed. "Thanks."

Ms. Wellesley offered her congratulations, too. "I guess this makes us teammates! And you and Ryan will be going to Dwyer next year. You'll do fine. Joe looks after his runners."

Others crowded around, filling the track. Then a race official came over. With pushing motions of both hands he shooed them off the track.

"The 3000's about to start," he said in teacherly tones. "Clear the track, please."

As the group moved toward the chain-link fence by the edge of the field, Matt's parents and Cathy-Marie pushed through, offering handshakes and hugs.

"Is that the one you called Ryan?" said Cathy-Marie, pointing at Ryan.

"Hard to miss, eh? Yeah, he's the coolest kid in school."

Cathy-Marie shook her head. "No, Matt, I think my brother is."

"Cool-o," said Ryan, who had overheard.

"*Cool-o?*" said Cathy-Marie in a whisper to her brother. "*Did he say, 'cool-o?*"

"It's lingo only real cool people use," said Ryan.

"Hey!" said Ashley. "We got this great idea. There's this race in, like, Bowmanville in a couple of weeks. It's a road race. Why don't we all go in it?"

"You mean the Alfie Shrubb Road Race?" said Tony. "That's a great run."

"Yeah, that might be it. Some old guy who used to run."

"Sounds like fun," said Matt. "That's important — the fun stuff."

"Life is mainly mud," said Tony. "You must learn to wallow in it."

Just then, Gavin Richards came through the gate from the lower soccer field. He was covered in mud from head to toe.

"What happened to you?" asked Ashley.

"I fell," said Gavin.

"Fell?"

"Well, a girl who likes me kind of gave me a push," he said, smiling.

Matt looked at Ashley, and at Gavin, then at Baz. They all laughed.

"Come on. Let's all go over and watch Ryan in the 3000 metres," said Ashley. "He's still part of the Lovey team."

They gathered on a bench in front of the grandstand by the track's edge. At the far side of the track, a starter's gun went *puff*, with a little wisp of smoke. A herd of runners started toward him.

Ryan, a head taller than almost all the others, stood out like a Popsicle.

Watching him move down the track, for a moment Matt wished that he had entered this event, too. *Oh, well*, he thought. *There would be other races*. That road race in Bowmanville with all of their group. That will be fun.

Beside him, Ashley smiled and squeezed his arm.

Other books you'll enjoy in the Sports Stories series

Track and Field

❏ *Mikayla's Victory* by Cynthia Bates #29

Mikayla must compete against her friend if she wants to represent her school at an important track event.

❏ *Walker's Runners* by Robert Rayner #55

Toby Morton hates gym. In fact, he doesn't run for anything — except the classroom door. Then Mr. Walker arrives and persuades Toby to join the running team.

Running

❏ *Fast Finish* by Bill Swan #30

Noah is a promising young runner headed for the provincial finals when he suddenly decides to withdraw from the event.

Baseball

❏ *Curve Ball* by John Danakas #1

Tom Poulos is looking forward to a summer of baseball in Toronto until his mother puts him on a plane to Winnipeg.

❏ *Baseball Crazy* by Martyn Godfrey #10

Rob Carter wins an all-expenses-paid chance to be bat boy at the Blue Jays spring training camp in Florida.

❏ *Shark Attack* by Judi Peers #25

The East City Sharks have a good chance of winning the county championship until their arch rivals get a tough new pitcher.

❏ *Hit and Run* by Dawn Hunter and Karen Hunter #35

Glen Thomson is a talented pitcher, but as his ego inflates, team morale plummets. Will he learn from being benched for losing his temper?

❏ *Power Hitter* by C. A. Forsyth #41

Connor's summer was looking like a write-off. That is, until he discovered his secret talent.

❏ *Sayonara, Sharks* by Judi Peers #48
In this sequel to *Shark Attack*, Ben and Kate are excited about the school trip to Japan, but Matt's not sure he wants to go.

Basketball

❏ *Fast Break* by Michael Coldwell #8
Moving from Toronto to small-town Nova Scotia was rough, but when Jeff makes the school basketball team he thinks things are looking up.

❏ *Camp All-Star* by Michael Coldwell #12
In this insider's view of a basketball camp, Jeff Lang encounters some unexpected challenges.

❏ *Nothing but Net* by Michael Coldwell #18
The Cape Breton Grizzly Bears prepare for an out-of-town basketball tournament they're sure to lose.

❏ *Slam Dunk* by Steven Barwin and Gabriel David Tick #23
In this sequel to *Roller Hockey Blues*, Mason Ashbury's basketball team adjusts to the arrival of some new players: girls.

❏ *Courage on the Line* by Cynthia Bates #33
After Amelie changes schools, she must confront difficult former teammates in an extramural match.

❏ *Free Throw* by Jacqueline Guest #34
Matthew Eagletail must adjust to a new school, a new team and a new father along with five pesky sisters.

❏ *Triple Threat* by Jacqueline Guest #38
Matthew's cyber-pal Free Throw comes to visit, and together they face a bully on the court.

❏ *Queen of the Court* by Michele Martin Bossley #40
What happens when the school's fashion queen winds up on the basketball court?

❏ *Shooting Star* by Cynthia Bates #46
Quyen is dealing with a troublesome teammate on her new basketball team, as well as trouble at home. Her parents seem haunted by something

that happened in Vietnam.

Soccer

❏ *Lizzie's Soccer Showdown* by John Danakas #3
When Lizzie asks why the boys and girls can't play together, she finds herself the new captain of the soccer team.

❏ *Alecia's Challenge* by Sandra Diersch #32
Thirteen-year-old Alecia has to cope with a new school, a new step-father, and friends who have suddenly discovered the opposite sex.

❏ *Shut-Out!* by Camilla Reghelini Rivers #39
David wants to play soccer more than anything, but will the new coach let him?

❏ *Offside!* by Sandra Diersch #43
Alecia has to confront a new girl who drives her teammates crazy.

❏ *Heads Up!* by Dawn Hunter and Karen Hunter #45
Do the Warriors really need a new, hot-shot player who skips practice?

❏ *Off the Wall* by Camilla Reghelini Rivers #52
Lizzie loves indoor soccer, and she's thrilled when her little sister gets into the sport. But when their teams are pitted against each other, Lizzie can only warn her sister to watch out.

❏ *Trapped!* by Michele Martin Bossley #53
There's a thief on Jane's soccer team, and everyone thinks it's her best friend, Ashley. Jane must find the true culprit to save both Ashley and the team's morale.